TELL ME TO FIGHT

CHARLOTTE BYRD

CHARLOTTE BYRD
dangerously addictive

Identifiers

ISBN (e-book): 978-1-63225-062-9

ISBN (paperback): 978-1-63225-063-6

ISBN (hardcover): 978-1-63225-064-3

ISBN (audio): 978-1-63225-077-3

❀ Created with Vellum

ABOUT TELL ME TO FIGHT
BOOK 5

I'm a man who takes what he wants.

What do I want? Her.

Olive Kernes owned me a debt and she thought that she had paid it back.

But now I want more.

I want more than just her time.

I want more than just her body.

Her new life has torn us apart.

Now, it's up to me to make things right.

I will make the pieces of our love fit back together if it's the last thing I do.

But can I do it in time?

Dive into the dangerous 5th book

of the new and addictive TELL ME
series by bestselling author
Charlotte Byrd.

PRAISE FOR CHARLOTTE BYRD

"Extremely captivating, sexy, steamy, intriguing, and intense!" ★★★★★

"Addictive and impossible to put down." ★★★★★

"I can't get enough of the turmoil, lust, love, drama, and secrets!" ★★★★★

"Fast-paced romantic suspense filled with twists and turns, danger, betrayal, and so much more." ★★★★★

"Decadent, delicious, & dangerously addictive!" - Amazon Review ★★★★★

"Titillation so masterfully woven, no reader can resist its pull. A MUST-BUY!" - Bobbi Koe, Amazon Review ★★★★★

"Captivating!" - Crystal Jones, Amazon Review ★★★★★

"Sexy, secretive, pulsating chemistry…" - Mrs. K, Amazon Reviewer ★★★★★

"Charlotte Byrd is a brilliant writer. I've read loads and I've laughed and cried. She writes a balanced book with brilliant characters. Well done!" -Amazon Review ★★★★★

"Hot, steamy, and a great storyline." - Christine Reese ★★★★★

"My oh my....Charlotte has made me a fan for life." - JJ, Amazon Reviewer ★★★★★

"Wow. Just wow. Charlotte Byrd leaves me speechless and humble… It definitely kept me on the edge of my seat. Once you pick it up, you won't put it down." - Amazon Review ★★★★★

" Intrigue, lust, and great characters...what more could you ask for?!" - Dragonfly Lady ★★★★★

DON'T MISS OUT!

Want to be the first to know about my upcoming sales, new releases and exclusive giveaways?

Bonus Points: Follow me on BookBub and Goodreads!

ALSO BY CHARLOTTE BYRD

All books are available at ALL major retailers! If you can't find it, please email me at charlotte@charlotte-byrd.com

Tell me Series
Tell Me to Stop
Tell Me to Go
Tell Me to Stay
Tell Me to Run
Tell Me to Fight
Tell Me to Lie

Tangled Series
Tangled up in Ice

Tangled up in Pain
Tangled up in Lace
Tangled up in Hate
Tangled up in Love

Black Series
Black Edge
Black Rules
Black Bounds
Black Contract
Black Limit

Lavish Trilogy
Lavish Lies
Lavish Betrayal
Lavish Obsession

Standalone Novels
Debt
Offer
Unknown
Dressing Mr. Dalton

1

NICHOLAS

WHERE THE TURQUOISE WATERS ARE WARM…

Here, the wind that comes off the ocean is warm and unoffensive. Instead of smacking you right in the face like it does in Massachusetts, it softly lures you into a state of utter relaxation.

Following the island's strict dress code of a t-shirt, shorts, and flip-flops, I walk the mile from my place to my favorite bar. I bury my feet in the cold fine sand underneath the table even before the bartender has the chance to take my order.

It's Wednesday evening, but days of the week don't have much meaning here. Each seat is filled with visitors from all over the English-speaking world. Some are only here for a week while others are here indefinitely. They are all here for different reasons except that they're not. They have put their old lives on hold to try something new.

I order a Belekin, a local light beer that only tastes good out in the salty air, and nod to Sammy and Greta out on the other side of the room. They are Swedish tourists in their late twenties who speak English without a hint of an accent.

I first spent the night with Sammy after we met dancing at the Lazy Lizard late one night. The following day, she introduced me to Greta and took up with a local. We spent the day sunbathing and swimming and then ended up back in my bed before sunrise.

I've been here long enough to know what the locals already know. One of the reasons single women come to this island is that it's a safe place to hook up with guys.

The men are friendly and with a population of around two thousand people, the place is about the size of a high school back home. Everyone knows everyone or at least almost everyone.

Perhaps I should've gone somewhere bigger, somewhere I could disappear a little easier but I'm not too worried.

I have a new name and a new identity. I'd been here once for a few days a long time ago and soon after Olive and I broke up this was the first place that came to mind.

Olive.

No matter how many drinks I have or how many women I sleep with, my mind keeps coming back to her.

The way Greta twists her hair around her finger is the exact same way that Olive used to do it.

The way that Sammy's eyes twinkle in the moonlight.

The way that Greta laughs.

The way that Sammy shuffles her feet.

The way that the girl down the street whose name I don't know shrugs her shoulders.

I see her everywhere I go.

She is like a ghost who haunts me.

"I'll take another, please," I say to Imogen, the bartender.

Imogen came here for a week from Vancouver, Canada, and never left.

She just cancelled the rest of her ticket, got a longer stay rental, and has been here for over six months.

To pay the rent, she tends bar at night and works as a dive instructor during the day.

She's nice and sweet and, surprisingly, impervious to my advances.

"When is Paul coming out?" I ask.

"In two days," she says with her face lighting up at the sound of her boyfriend's name.

"You think you'll be able to get him to stay?" I ask.

I know she wants him to, and I also know that he has his reservations.

"I hope so," Imogen says, making three drinks at once.

Paul is a computer engineer and there aren't many jobs in his field around here.

According to her, this is the biggest obstacle in their relationship.

She wants to stay here indefinitely and he wants to live the normal life they had back in Vancouver. Their situation is the perfect example of irreconcilable differences but I don't have the heart to tell her that it's probably not going to work out.

"I hope so, too," I say, finishing the second beer.

Due to the plethora of British expats, soccer tends to dominate the screens and today is no exception.

After ordering another beer, I make my way in between the tables toward the bathroom.

My eyes drift over the room and at the second television near the window. That's when I see it.

It's a picture of me with my real name and the word *Wanted* on the top.

My heart jumps into my chest, but I keep walking.

Right before I disappear behind the corner, I see Art Hedison giving an interview.

I rush into the bathroom and find an

empty stall. Locking the door, I try to figure out what to do.

"What the fuck is going on?" I whisper under my breath.

No, no, no, no. This isn't happening.

I take a few deep breaths to calm myself down and then exit the room.

I already ordered a beer and I still need to pay my tab so I can't just walk out without drawing even more attention to myself.

"Hey, do you mind if I change the channel?" I ask the group of couples doing shots underneath the TV with my face on it.

None of them are watching it and I already have my finger on the remote when a tall guy nearby gives me a brief nod of approval.

I flip it to another soccer game, knowing that at least one patron will object if anyone were to change it in the future.

When I get to the bar, I give the beer that has been waiting for me to the girl who takes a seat to my right. Normally, I would make small talk and try to get her to come home with me but not tonight.

"See you later, Imogen!" I yell, leaving her a generous tip.

"You leaving already?" She calls back to me when I'm already near the front door.

"Something came up." I shrug casually and leave.

2

NICHOLAS

WHEN I TRY TO FIGURE OUT MY NEXT MOVE...

W alking back to my cabin, I revel in the way the breeze kisses my skin ever so lightly. This is the last time that I will feel this in a very long time. There are other islands I can go to, but none of them will be Caye Caulker, Belize.

My flip-flops make a loud smacking sound as they hit the back of my heels. There are no roads here, not any official ones anyway.

No cars either.

People get around mainly on foot or by bike and the occasional golf cart. This place exists somewhere between the past and the present.

The internet is fast but the pace of the world is slow. There isn't much to do but swim, snorkel, dive, fish, read, eat, talk, and drink. Isn't that kind of perfect, though?

That's exactly why I came here. I need to get away from everything.

I thought I could leave the bad out there, somewhere back in Boston but now it has followed me here.

Now, the asshole who I helped and who made promises to me is now on television talking about how dangerous I am.

This is my way out I think, gritting my teeth as regret and anger bubble up within me.

"Hey there, stranger," Ali, the French expat, says as I walk past her apartment and head toward mine.

We haven't hooked up because she has been out of town the majority of the time that I've been here. That and I've also had some reservations about sleeping with someone who lives so close to me.

"You want to come over for a bottle of

wine?" she asks.

"Maybe some other time," I say, giving her a brief wave.

Back inside my one bedroom cabin with minimal furnishings, not as a result of any particular decorating intention, I turn on the television and start to pack.

I can't find the program that was on at the bar so I Google my name.

The first thing to show up are the videos.

I am the focus of at least three different national programs and Art is interviewed by the hosts of each one.

"What a fuckin' asshole," I say, shaking my head and grabbing the suitcase out of the closet.

I fold just a few shirts and pants along with my one pair of loafers and toss in my toiletries. In the bottom cupboard right next to the sink, I pull out an envelope with all of my passports. Thanks to a contact from back home, I have a number of them, but I'm not entirely sure which one I should use.

"Don't forget, he is charming but very

dangerous." I hear Art say in the background. "He is the main suspect responsible for killing his ex-partner—"

I close the video.

I've had enough of his ugly face and his ugly lies.

Why is he doing this to me? I wonder. Now?

I shake my head and let out a small laugh. It's not a big mystery, though. They must have gotten something on him and this was his way out.

It's either that or he's just doing this to screw me, I decide, letting out a deep sigh.

"Well, fuck you, Art, I'm not going down that easily."

I grab my suitcase and take one last look around the place. I will miss it here.

I hope that when all of this blows over, I can come back. This isn't going to be the last time I'm here.

The golf cart masquerading as a cab meets me outside my door and takes me to the ferry terminal where I get onto the last boat going to Belize City.

The waters are choppy and I bounce

around the plastic seat below deck the whole way there. Half an hour later, when I get onto solid ground, I feel sick to my stomach but I'm not sure if the bumpy boat ride is the sole culprit.

I'm tempted to get a hotel in town and get some rest but I decide against it. This country is English-speaking and the majority of the television programs are piped in directly from the United States.

No, it's much better for me to get into Mexico as soon as possible. Mexico is a huge country where it's much easier to get lost than in Belize.

I take an actual cab to the bus terminal and buy a ticket to Merida, Mexico. Twenty minutes later, I climb onto the pristine ADO express bus along with all of the other passengers and put on a sweatshirt as soon as I take a seat. I stare out of the window, wondering how I can't see my breath in this extremely air-conditioned vehicle. After everyone's bags are stowed and locked away underneath, we take off.

I have cell reception for a little bit of

the way, enough to find out that I have become quite a crime celebrity. Everyone is suddenly consumed with the case of what happened to my partner and there are a number of podcasts devoted to his missing persons case.

This is unusual given that most of these shows focus on missing attractive blonde women in their twenties who disappear under unusual circumstances. My partner's case is neither unusual nor suspicious.

He worked for the mob. He stole jewelry and other expensive products. When he started to work for himself, the mob got angry and decided to take him out. It's a story as old as time and yet thanks to Art now suddenly everyone is concerned and everyone thinks I did it.

My reception goes away just as the roads go from bumpy to practically impassable. I turn on an audiobook and stare out of the window into the Belizian jungle. Besides the bus's headlights, there are no lights illuminating the road. I close my eyes and try to relax.

3

NICHOLAS

WHEN THERE ARE COMPLICATIONS...

The following morning, I take a cab from the bus terminal and spend the day in a hotel waiting for my flight. After a long nap and a big dinner at the downstairs restaurant, I feel somewhat rested and prepared.

No, prepared is not the right word. Just rested.

It's one thing to cross over from Belize to Mexico on a fake passport and it's a whole other thing to do so from Mexico to an international location like Thailand.

On top of that, there's a warrant out for my arrest and they are showing my face on television screens across the country. If there is even one crime show junkie at the airport then I'm totally fucked.

I don't want to think of today as the last day of my life, but just in case it is and I'm arrested I want to be well-fed.

"Was everything to your liking?" the waitress asks.

"Yes, it was excellent," I say. "Where are you from?"

"Houston," she says with a smile.

She has long golden hair and green eyes. Tall and thin, she looks nothing like Olive yet everything about her reminds me of her.

We flirt for a few minutes and I stay for a few more drinks. When she leaves to take care of her other customers, my phone dings.

It's from my bank. The payment didn't go through and they've cancelled my ticket.

Shit.

I re-read the email again, trying to figure out what could've happened.

I didn't have a chance to set up a credit

card yet under a new name, but there's plenty of money in my bank account.

I put in my password and wait as the page loads.

My account has been frozen.

Shit.

Shit.

Shit.

I shake my head. No, this can't be happening. This isn't under my real name. How could they have this identity?

The waitress brings me the bill and I pause.

If I give them this card, the payment isn't going to go through.

I search for some cash in my wallet, knowing full well that I don't have any pesos.

"I'm so sorry, I'm having some issue with my bank right now."

She stares at me.

"I'm sorry. I wouldn't have eaten here if I knew that but I can't access my account for some reason."

She shakes her head.

"Can I pay you in American dollars?"

She laughs.

"What can I do?" I say, showing her the fifty.

She takes a deep breath as I wait. I have another card but I can't risk using it in case it's frozen, too.

I have to first check the account online.

She taps her foot on the floor before finally giving me a big shrug and tossing her hair back.

"This happens sometimes with our customers," she explains. "I will have to charge you a surcharge for paying in dollars."

"Yes, of course." I let out a sigh of relief.

For a second, I thought she might call the police and then I'd be in the middle of a real shit storm.

I pay an extra ten dollars for the courtesy and give her a big tip on top of that. But I forgo getting another drink because I don't have much money left.

When I get upstairs, I log into the computer and realize that all of my accounts are frozen. I don't have access to anything. I have this room until tomorrow night but after that, I don't even know how I could afford to pay for a night's stay.

The doorbell rings.

My heart jumps into my throat.

I make a fist and brace myself for what's to come. Turning around, I look out of the window. I'm on the eighth floor and the drop is straight down. If those are the cops, the only way out of this place is directly through them.

"It's me," a quiet feminine voice says through the door. "Mallory."

"Hi." I swing the door open to the waitress from earlier tonight.

"I don't normally do this…" she says, looking down at the floor.

"Come in, please." I lock the door quickly behind her. "It's nice to have more time with you. I wasn't sure if I was coming on a bit too strong there…at your place of business."

She wraps her hands around her shoulders and says nothing.

"I wasn't sure if you were just flirting with me to get a bigger tip," I joke.

"Not exactly." She laughs. "Though I did appreciate it."

"Well, I appreciate you helping me out. I am in quite a little jam right now."

"Oh, you are?" she asks, raising her eyebrows.

I nod, trying to decide how much I should disclose.

On one hand, it's probably best to keep her out of it, but on the other she's the only person that I know in this town and she's probably the only one I could borrow a few dollars from before I can figure something out.

But that's not why I had offered her a drink and that's not why I want her to stay.

She flips her hair from one side to another and tilts her head toward mine. It's undeniable, Mallory is quite easy on the eyes.

Besides, I started hating being alone after Olive. She tends to haunt me the most when I'm alone. It got so bad at one point that the only way I could get any sleep was with a stranger lying next to me.

"How long are you in town?" Mallory asks when I hand her a shot of tequila.

"Well, I was supposed to leave tonight but now I'm not sure. I have some things to work out with the bank."

"The bank is closed," she says, taking a sip.

"Yes, I know." I give her a nod. "I can't do anything until tomorrow."

I move a few inches closer to her and put my glass down.

She looks up at me.

I press my lips to hers and she kisses me back.

We are hungry for each other and our clothes come off one by one.

I lose myself in the moment until she whispers "Eric," the name I gave her.

When I glance at her below me, her face disappears and she becomes Olive.

4

OLIVE

WHEN WE DISAPPEAR...

I n the mornings, I dress in layers, which I slowly shed throughout the day.

I wake up around eight and after half an hour of lounging in bed, I get dressed and go on a walk. There are tall mountains right outside our house, one with a peak of about ten thousand feet.

The neighbors told me that in the winter, it's covered in snow and down here in the valley the temperature is still in the seventies and the sky is as blue as it has ever been.

Palm trees line my two mile walk since almost every house has one or two in their front yard. This is an older part of the city, meaning that it was built up in the 1950s and the architecture is what they call mid-century modern.

All of the houses, including ours, are one level, about two thousand square feet, some much more. The backyards come with ample green space with hedges to ensure privacy from prying eyes. The majority also have pools and hot tubs.

The ceilings inside are relatively tall but not as cathedral-like as the ones in the older house back east. We have a vaulted ceiling in our rental with a big window looking out onto the street outside. The place is furnished with low to the floor mid-century style furniture to complete the look. Just about the only thing that makes it feel like it's 2020 is the sixty-inch television mounted on the wall.

After my walk, on which I say hello to at least five dogs and their owners, I get straight into the pool.

This is one of the driest places in the United States, if not the world, with humidity often hovering around fifteen percent. We heat the pool to eighty-five, which sounds like it would be lukewarm but it's actually not at all. Due to the dryness of the air, the pool is just refreshing enough and actually quite cold when you get out of it.

After swimming for a bit, I dry myself off with a towel, which takes about a few seconds, and sit down with a book on the lounger. The cushion is incredibly soft and it's curved to mold to the human body making it particularly comfortable. If there is such a thing as paradise, this is it.

When I first imagined going to California, I tried to brace my expectations. There is no way that it would be, or could be, as amazing as I had imagined it.

Yes, there would be sunshine.

Yes, there would be comfortable weather all year around.

Yes, there is not many bugs, nor is there any freezing black snow to clear off the car.

But everything couldn't be that perfect, right?

Something would have to be off.

Little did I know how much more wonderful it would really be.

The food is better quality and the restaurants serve unique and delicious entrees.

The people are nice, and polite, and friendly.

Everyone seems happy.

It reminds me of one of the first days in May when it's just warm enough for everyone to get outside and enjoy life and for that one brief day everyone in the city seems content and happy. Well, it's like that here all the time.

When I get a little bit too hot in the sun, I change out of my bathing suit and grab my iPad. Our rental has a swinging chair in the corner of the backyard that is typically in the shade. It's lined with pillows and a faux sheepskin rug.

I put my feet on the soft ottoman in front of it and swing myself as I read. Time passes slowly and yet quickly. Before I know it, it's the afternoon and I've finished my book.

Later that evening, when the sun starts to set, I put on my running shoes and go for a little jog. Before I got here, I hadn't run in years.

But the days are long and it's nice to fill them with some physical activity. When I started a few weeks ago, I couldn't even run a third of a mile but now I can do two.

My lungs are burning but I take my time and go as far as I can.

I used to get stitches in my sides, but not anymore.

I don't run very fast but I'm proud of the work that I'm doing.

I meet the same dog owners that I'd met earlier that day only this time our interaction is just a cursory wave. I want to kneel down and pet each one but that would make me break momentum and I've learned that in this kind of thing momentum is everything.

Back home, sweaty and red-faced, I change into my bathing suit in the master bedroom with a sliding door that faces the backyard and jump into the pool to cool off.

"You swimming again?" Owen walks out with a beer in hand.

"Don't you just love it?" I ask.

Owen shrugs.

When we first got here, he swam all the time but months later the novelty has worn off.

It hasn't for me.

Actually, I doubt it ever will.

If I were to buy a house, I now know that a pool and a hot tub are a must.

"Can't believe that you're still swimming this much," he says, shaking his head.

"Can't believe you're still drinking this much," I point out.

When we first got here, we indulged a bit in having a few too many drinks but after a while I got sick of waking up with pounding headaches.

After I quit, Owen started drinking more.

Now, I hardly ever see him without a beer in his hand.

"At least, I don't drink anything too strong," he says.

"Yeah, I guess. But I'm not sure it's such a good idea to drink during the day at all."

He shrugs and hangs his head.

I know that he hates me bringing this up.

But what else do I do when I see him going downhill? Should I not try to stop him at all? Should I not try to put on the brakes even a little bit?

I climb out of the pool and wrap the towel around myself.

My skin gets covered in goose bumps until I dry off.

"You know that I don't mean anything by saying that, right?" I ask. "I'm just worried. I don't want things to get out of hand."

"Don't be," Owen says. "What…do you think I'm going to become an alcoholic or something?"

"It's possible." I nod. "It happens."

"Well, not to me."

"It's a disease, Owen. There's nothing to be ashamed of. And it's progressive so if you keep this up, after a while you won't be able to stop."

His eyes turn ice cold as he clenches his jaw. He's about to say something back to me but he chooses to keep it to himself.

I head inside through my bedroom, but Owen calls back out to me right before I slide the door closed.

"Oh, hey, I think you might want to come out and see what they're showing on TV," he says.

"What is it?"

"It's about Nicholas."

5

OLIVE

WHEN I SEE HIM AGAIN…

I don't know exactly what Owen means and I don't really want to know. I'm tired of him making me feel bad about Nicholas. I have a lot of regrets about my life but falling for him doesn't even come close to making the cut.

He burst into my life like a wildfire and destroyed almost everything. Yet just like a wildfire, his presence gave me the opportunity to start my life again.

On my terms.

I'm angry with Nicholas.

Pissed.

Upset.

Disappointed.

But the more time passes, the more I miss him.

I hate how much time I have wasted.

He lied to me and yet now all of these months later, I sort of think that I allowed it.

I didn't press him hard enough.

I didn't challenge all of those things that I should have.

I get dressed slowly, putting on the layers that I typically wear in the mornings and evenings when the outside temperatures drop by about twenty degrees.

Before leaving my room, I take a deep breath and steady my mind.

Nicholas is not an easy topic of conversation between Owen and me.

Owen sees nothing but the worst in him.

He believes he killed his girlfriend and his partner and he knows that he betrayed him, us, and he will use any opportunity to rub it in my face.

"Don't you remember our pact?" I ask, walking into the living room where Owen is sprawled out on the couch with a big smile on his face.

He is so drunk that he can barely keep his eyes open yet the beer in his hand remains perfectly vertical.

"And that is?" he asks.

"That we're not going to bring him up again."

"Well, if that's what you want," Owen says slowly, slurring his words just a bit. "I just thought that you might be interested in what they're saying on the news about him."

I furrow my brow and turn toward the television.

There are huge blown up pictures of him in a suit with the words Nicholas Crawford right below.

I bring my hand to my lips unwilling to believe my eyes.

Owen unpauses the television and America's Fugitives starts to run.

The narrator explains how Nicholas used to work for one of the biggest organized crime syndicates in the Northeast until he and his partner decided to break away, do some deals on their own, and keep their boss out of the loop.

The program doesn't reveal many names besides Nicholas' nor does it go into anything beyond the generalities.

What it does offer is an interview with Art Hedison who discussed in detail how dangerous Nicholas is and that the FBI now needs the public's help in locating him.

"That asshole," I say, shaking my head. "He fuckin' betrayed him. We did that job to help him and here he is on primetime…"

My words trail off as anger starts to bubble up.

"No, Nicholas is the asshole," Owen says. "He should've known better than to trust the FBI. He should've known better than to inform on us."

He uses the word *us*, when it's really just *him*.

I haven't done anything.

I never turned on anyone and I don't owe anyone any debts.

"I just can't believe that he's a fugitive now," I say with a sigh.

For the first time ever, I'm actually afraid that something bad is going to happen to Nicholas.

Before, all of my worries were so focused on Owen and now there is suddenly another man in my life to worry about.

The FBI are after him.

His face is all over the news.

When I search his name on my phone, I realize that he's the criminal of the hour.

There are podcasts and YouTube episodes from indie producers devoted to his case.

"Why are you so upset about this?" Owen asks. "He had this coming."

"How can you even ask me that?" I say.

"How can I not? He betrayed you. He fucked you over."

"No, he lied. He shouldn't have, but he was in a jam. He didn't have a choice."

"You're such a fucking idiot," Owen says. "How long will it take you to get it through your thick head that he is a con artist and a liar and he never gave a fuck about you."

I take a deep breath.

I hate it when he talks to me like this.

He's drunk.

That's not an excuse but he would never talk to me like this sober.

Engaging with Owen even more would just make things worse and yet I can't help it.

"Who the fuck do you think you are?" I ask as sternly as possible, balling up my hands into fists. "Don't talk to me like that."

"Okay, I'm sorry, Olive. Please," he says quickly, his words rushing over one another. "I just hate how you still care about him. Don't you get it? Art is a dick but he's telling us the truth. He killed his partner. They have a case on him."

I inhale deeply.

I don't actually know if he did kill his partner and given his line of work, it's a real possibility that he did.

"And my girlfriend. He killed her, too. They'll prove it one day, you'll see."

I shake my head and cross my arms.

"You don't believe me?" Owen asks.

He looks wounded, like I had just shot him in the heart.

"I don't know, Owen," I give in a little.

He's too drunk to have a normal conversation, but there's no way that I would ever bring this up when he's sober.

"This is just the beginning of finding out the truth about him, Olive. He's charming and cool but he's a terrible person. I know that you'll come around someday."

I hate his certainty, and I hate my uncertainty.

I wish I could just believe him and not believe everything that they are saying about him.

But I don't.

I don't have any good reason or evidence, just my heart.

That's enough, right?

For now, it has to be.

6

OLIVE
WHEN I MEET A STRANGER…

I have always been cold for as long as I can remember.

My hands and feet are particularly susceptible, especially in the mornings.

I just happened to mention it to a woman who lives a few doors down. It turns out that she has a PhD in Natural Medicine and it was she who mentioned that I should look into having my thyroid checked.

If I didn't want to go to the doctor then I could take a thermometer and record my temperature every morning for three days in a row, soon after sleep and before going to the bathroom or making any movements at all. Then I had to add up the number and divide by three. If my body temperature was below ninety-eight degrees then I had a poorly-functioning thyroid.

When I got home and did a lot more research about this online, I discovered that I actually checked a number of different boxes regarding this issue.

I am always cold.

I am often tired for no reason whatsoever.

My hair seems to be thinning.

My skin is dry.

I have trouble losing weight even though I had been following a pretty strict Keto diet (in addition, substituting fish for meat and avoiding dairy).

My neighbor also mentioned that even though normally nuts are a good thing to have, they are quite fattening, especially walnuts, and if I had too many of them, they would slow down my thyroid function even more.

Furthermore, a few months ago, I cut out all salt thinking that my problem was that I was retaining too much water. Well, it turns out salt is essential for people with underperforming thyroids and that seemed to slow mine down even more.

All of this seemed to explain why my weight hasn't budged even though I've put in a lot of effort to lose a few pounds over the last couple weeks.

Today is the third day of me taking thyroid supplements along with iron and iodine drops. I am still cold in the mornings but not as much as I used to be. And I've noticed that I have a lot more energy throughout the day.

In addition to supplements, I've also changed my diet to more plant-based and have been making myself green juice every morning. I was never a big fan of vegetables but suddenly I have developed a taste for them.

I put on my running shoes and head to the kitchen to make my juice. I cut up two stalks of celery, a cucumber, add dill and parsley along with two scoops of organic pea protein from Trader Joe's. After adding a cup of water, half a lemon, and salt, I tighten the lid and start the blender.

"Hey!" someone yells over the cacophony of sound.

The voice startles me and I jump away from the counter with my heart in my throat.

"Oh my God, I didn't mean to scare you," the woman says with a concerned look on her face.

"No, I'm sorry," I say, shaking my head and trying to get my breathing under control.

She's about my age with long dark hair and olive skin.

Owen's Metallica t-shirt looks like a dress on her.

Her legs are bare as are her feet.

She introduces herself as Shelly, shaking my hand and adjusting her shirt as she talks.

"I'm a waitress at the Fire Lounge," Shelly says, rubbing the front of her foot with the heel of another.

"It's nice to meet you," I say. "Do you want some coffee?"

"No, thanks, but I'd love some of that juice."

"Yes, of course," I say, pouring half of it in a cup for her.

"Are you sure? I only want this if you have more."

"I've got plenty of veggies in the fridge. It's really not a problem."

"I just love having this kind of thing in the morning but I'm always too lazy to make it myself. So, I end up going to Jamba Juice."

"Yeah, it's a bit of a pain, at first, but you get used to it," I say.

We take a few sips listening to the silence. I like her being here.

Sometimes having a lot of one-on-one time with Owen gets a bit exhausting. I hope she will stay for the rest of the day.

"Can I ask you something?" Shelly asks, wiping the green mustache off her lips.

I nod.

"Does your brother do this kind of thing…a lot?"

"What do you mean?"

"Bring someone home from the bar?"

"No," I say, shaking my head.

"That's what he told me but you know how it is, they all say that," Shelly says, shrugging. "I've said it myself about a thousand times."

We both laugh.

"You like him, huh?" I ask.

She nods and looks down at the floor as if she had just admitted something embarrassing.

"No, he doesn't do this often," I say. "Actually, we've been living here for a few months now and he has never brought a girl home before."

"Really?" Her eyes light up in disbelief.

I give her a shrug and a wink.

We both hang our hopes on Owen.

Shelly wants him to like her as much as she likes him and I do, too. I have a feeling that a girlfriend is exactly what would make Owen a little bit less intense with me.

It will divert his attention away from me, and maybe having someone he enjoys spending time with will make him drink a little less, too.

Owen comes out of his room, wearing only shorts. He gives Shelly a little peck on the cheek and then wraps his arm around her shoulder.

"Hey, girls," he says. "Whatcha talking about?"

"Your ears burning?" I ask.

Shelly smiles and looks down at the floor.

He brushes hair out of her face and gives her another kiss, this time on the mouth.

A wave of relief washes over me.

He likes her. He really likes her!

"You two have any plans for today?" I nudge them.

"I don't know, maybe we'll grab some brunch. My day is pretty open," Owen says, turning to Shelly.

"I don't have to be at work until nine so we can do…whatever." Her eyes twinkle at the thought of spending it with him.

"You want to come?" Owen offers.

"No, I'm good, you two have fun."

When I head out on my walk, I can't help but smile.

This is it.

He met a nice girl and she's going to take him out of that dark place he has been in ever since we got here.

Closing the door behind me, I glance back.

Owen still has his arm around Shelly but his eyes glare at mine.

7

OLIVE

WHEN I LOOK THROUGH THE FILE...

I spend the following morning lounging around in bed way past the time when I should get up.

It feels nice not to stick to the schedule that I had set out for myself and to just take a little break. After finishing another book, my thoughts wander back to the folder that Nicholas gave me.

He said he was waiting for the right time to give it to me but it never presented itself. Why the hell not?

I don't know how long he has had the file but it must've been ages. There were so many times that I had cried on his shoulder trying to figure out what to do and where to go from here.

I have a lot of things to be angry with him for and this is the one that probably pisses me off the most.

Why did he wait?

Why didn't he just tell me?

I open the folder and read through the contents for what feels like the millionth time.

I know her name.

I know some about her family history.

I know that she came from a wealthy family.

Most importantly, I know where she lives. Right here, in Palm Springs, California.

When it was time to decide where we should start our new lives, Owen had many suggestions, but I only had one.

My real mother lives in Palm Springs and that's the only place I wanted to go.

He has no idea that that's why I insisted on coming here. I played up the sunshine and the palm trees and the eternal summer but I downplayed one important reason.

Why did I do that?

I'm not sure if Owen would've come with me here otherwise.

It's not that he isn't interested in finding my mother, I just have a feeling that he would've objected.

And how does that saying go again?

It's easier to beg forgiveness than ask permission?

I didn't want to have yet another thing to fight with him about.

I didn't want him to say no, so I never asked.

What Owen does know is her name and basic things about her.

I would've happily kept the folder to myself but I was too distraught to hide it when he came back into my room. I was also too angry and disappointed.

So, he has seen some of the pages but not the one at the end.

Not the one with her address on it. Otherwise, he'd know that she lives exactly 3.4 miles away from us.

I get sick of lounging and decide to finally get some fresh air and go on a hike.

I'm getting bored running up and down the same streets all the time so last night I downloaded the All Trails app that shows all of the hikes around me.

Much to my surprise, there are over five hundred hikes in the Coachella Valley. There are at least five that are within five miles of the house.

I grab my water bottle, a small Ziploc bag of walnuts and sunflower seeds, and my phone. Less than ten minutes later, I'm going on my first hike.

The trail starts off at the visitors' center where they show me a map of where I'm headed. The desert floor is cloaked with creosote bushes. Some are short but others can be as tall as nine feet in height. When I bend down to look at one's dark leaves, I notice it smells a bit like rain.

The trail takes me further away from civilization, down the valley below, and higher into the folds of the mountains.

Once I make it around the bend, large

boulders that are taller than I am line the trail as if they are the welcoming gate inviting me in.

The trail loops higher and higher and before the city below disappears entirely. I turn around and take a look at it one last time.

Up here, the mountains are tan and red, but looking down at the city all I see is a wall of green.

There are so many palm trees lining the streets that the entire valley looks as if it is a tropical rainforest.

When the trail gets even steeper and I have to scramble over some rocks, my phone vibrates. I'm listening to an audiobook and plan on just ignoring the call but then I see who it's from, Sydney.

We haven't talked for a while and I miss her.

"Hey!" I say, huffing and trying to catch my breath.

She immediately presses the FaceTime button and even though now I'm totally regretting my decision to answer her call, I have no choice.

"Oh my God, where are you?" she asks in her bubbly voice.

I flip the phone around and show her the mountains that wrap around me.

"That place is insane," Sydney says.

"I know, right?"

"So, what are you doing?"

I turn the phone back to me and try not to focus on my red, sweaty face in the upper right hand corner.

"I'm taking a hike. This canyon is only ten minutes away and I thought I would check it out."

"I wish I was there," she says.

"Me, too!"

"So, I guess you're a super healthy California girl now, huh?" she jokes.

I nod.

"It's disgusting." I nod. "You should see me. I'm having green smoothies made from vegetables multiple times a day and I'm running, and swimming, and, apparently, hiking now!"

"You make me sick!" She laughs.

"You need to come visit and rescue me from becoming the super me."

"I will!"

Sydney doesn't know exactly where I am, but she does know that I'm in California.

Perhaps I should be more careful and not FaceTime with her just in case but I know that she'll never tell anyone a thing.

I ask her about how she has been but she only briefly glosses over it before getting to the real reason she has called.

"I saw Nicholas on TV," she says.

"Yeah, me, too," I say with a huff just as a stitch in my side starts to act up.

Getting tired, I drop my hand down away from my face.

"Are you okay?"

"Yeah, I'm fine." I stop trying to walk and talk into the camera at the same time. "I saw him, too."

"What does this mean?"

"I don't know. I guess that the FBI is after him."

"They are saying he killed his partner," she whispers.

"He didn't," I say.

"Are you sure?"

"Yes, he did *not* do that, Syd."

As much as I want to tell her the details of what we did at that house together, she doesn't know much about that and the less she knows the better.

She doesn't know that Nicholas was working as an informer for the FBI and she doesn't know that he was giving them information on Owen.

She does know that a few bad people are after Owen for what he said in prison and they want him dead.

And she does know that Nicholas and I broke up.

We talk about it for a while as I scramble higher and higher and then suddenly the reception starts to go out. We are forced to cut our conversation short and I promise to call her back as soon as I get home.

An hour later, I walk into my room, drenched in sweat and find Owen sitting on the edge of my bed reading the file about my mother.

8

OLIVE

WHEN HE DISCOVERS MY SECRET…

"What are you doing here?" I ask, holding onto the door handle for support.

"What is this?" he asks, turning his body toward me.

"What are you doing in my room? Why are you going through my stuff?" I demand to know.

He shrugs innocently and licks his lips.

Buying time, perhaps?

Or just trying to figure out what to say?

"I was just trying to find out a little bit more about your mom. You were so… secretive with this thing."

"I wasn't secretive—" I start to say defensively.

"Then why didn't you tell me the truth?"

Owen narrows his eyes.

I can't tell how many beers he has had today but I'm certain that he isn't completely sober.

"About what?" I ask.

"About this!" He rises to his feet, shoving the folder in the air.

I finally unclasp my hand away from the doorknob, take a few steps closer to him, and grab the folder out of his hand.

"I want you to leave," I say quietly but with certainty.

"I'm not going to leave until we talk about this." He sits back down, crossing his arms. "I'm not going to leave until you tell me why you wanted to come here."

"You already know," I whisper.

"I want to hear it from your lips."

"What? What do you want to know?"

"The truth!" he roars.

I wait until silence falls between us again before saying another word.

"Fine," I give in.

He already knows so why fight him on this?

"I wanted to come to Palm Springs because this is where my real mother lives," I say quietly.

He doesn't reply.

"You happy now?" I challenge him.

"Why didn't you tell me? You didn't think I would understand?"

"No, that's not it."

"So, why?"

"I wasn't sure how you were going to react and I didn't want to get into it. I didn't want you to write this place off because I want to meet her."

"So, you didn't meet her yet?"

"No," I say.

"Why not?"

I don't say anything.

Instead, I slouch and look down at my shoes.

A bead of sweat rolls off my forehead and lands on the floor.

"Because I'm afraid," I say after a moment.

He stares at me in disbelief.

"We have been here this whole time and you haven't even tried to go and see her?"

"No," I say, shaking my head. "I will, I just need more time. More courage. I don't know. More of something."

His anger toward me seems to dissipate but I can't say the same thing about mine.

These last two months have been more than just a little challenging and Owen hasn't been doing anything to make it any better.

He's drinking.

He's telling me what to do, no, he's bullying me around.

I walk on pins and needles around him, afraid to say something offensive out of fear of his rage.

He has never raised his hand to me but his words hurt like hell.

And this?

Finding him here in my room going through my personal things?

What gives him the right to do that?

Oh, yes, of course, me.

I'm the one setting boundaries, or the lack thereof.

"Why were you in my room?" I ask.

My voice is soft but firm.

This conversation isn't going to be about me answering questions for once, it's going to be about *him*.

"I don't know," he says after a moment. "I guess I came here looking for something."

"You can't do that."

"I know."

"No, you don't," I insist. "Otherwise, we wouldn't be having this conversation."

"I'm sorry, okay?" Owen says. "What else do you want me to say?"

"I don't know, but it doesn't sound like you're sorry. Not at all," I say, shaking my head.

I run my finger over the grain of the dresser. The wood is smooth and polished. On the surface it looks pristine. But when you look a little bit closer, when you touch it, you can feel it. Some would say that these kind of imperfections make it look real, but I would argue why does life have to be all about faults and deficiencies and mistakes? Or is that just my life?

Owen and I talk for a bit but the conversation just goes in circles.

He apologizes over and over yet none of his apologies feel genuine.

Even if they were, I don't care.

I'm tired.

I'm sick of being here with *him*.

Even though I just got back from an arduous hike, I go out again. The sun is still high in the sky beating down on my already tired body. I take a few sips from my water bottle, but my thirst is only quenched temporarily.

"What am I going to do?" I ask myself out loud.

The street is deserted except for one car somewhere far in the distance.

I keep walking.

There is something about movement that clears my head.

I want to go to my room and curl up in my bed but his presence in my room has tainted my sacred space.

It's not that I don't love Owen anymore.

He's still my brother.

It's just that I can't bear to live with him.

It's a two-bedroom house and yet when he's home, which is pretty often, he seems to suck up all of the oxygen in the place.

A lot of that has to do with his drinking.

At first, we drank to celebrate.

Then he drank because he's bored.

And now? Now, I suspect he drinks because he has to.

My foot collides with the pavement in an odd way and I trip, nearly losing my balance.

Suddenly, it hits me.

We came all the way out here, three thousand miles away, to start a new life but neither of us has.

Normal lives involve jobs and friends and some sort of regular rhythm to the day.

Perhaps one of the reasons why he's so

bored and why he's drinking so much is that he doesn't have anything else to do.

He likes to read and when he was in prison that was pretty much all he had.

And now? He needs more.

But what about me?

I could try to get another content writing job or some other educational writing position.

Or maybe I can work in a tutoring center?

Despite all of my education, that was never really what I wanted to do and now having some money and no actual need to get that job, I don't really want to do it.

Still, I need to do something.

But what?

9

OLIVE

WHEN HE MAKES AMENDS…

I brace myself for more conflict when the sun starts to set and I have no choice but to come back home.

I take a deep breath before I walk through the door and am pleasantly surprised to find Owen in the kitchen cooking.

The table in the dining room is fully set for two including placements, wine glasses, plates, utensils, and napkins.

I had no idea we even had placements or napkins.

"Where did you find all this stuff?"

"In the cabinet right here." He points

to the bottom row right next to the dishwasher.

I look at the stove and see that he's making salmon, cauliflower rice, and asparagus.

"So, what's the occasion?" I ask.

"Just wanted to formally apologize for what I did and start again. Blank page and all."

I nod.

After changing out of my dirty clothes, I come out to him plating my dinner.

He pours me a glass of wine and tops off his own.

I'm not sure how much he has had to drink today but he doesn't seem as lethargic and intoxicated as normal.

The food tastes delicious and I appreciate the effort.

When he smacks his lips proud of his own creation, I laugh.

"There you go," he says. "I missed that."

"What?"

"You laughing. I feel like we haven't laughed in ages."

"We haven't," I agree.

We take a few more bites.

I take another sip of wine.

"I've been thinking about something," I say with hesitation.

He looks up at me and waits.

"We're in this new place, new town, new coast to start our new lives. But we're not really doing that."

"What do you mean?"

"Well, it feels a lot like we're just here on…vacation," I pause, waiting for the right word.

He gives me a slight nod to keep going.

"Doesn't it?" I ask. "I mean, we don't really do anything. We don't work, we don't have friends…I think that's why we're having these issues."

I intentionally avoid using the word "you" even though that's what I mean.

It's not that I don't have issues but my issue right now is mainly him.

"Yeah, I've been thinking about that myself," Owen says, rubbing his chin. "It's a little boring to not do anything all day, isn't it?"

"Yeah, a bit."

"It's not like we exactly need money but sometimes that poses even more issues. Like, suddenly, we're forced to decide what it is that we really want to do with our lives."

Owen finishes one last bite and leaves his fork and knife on the plate.

"What kind of job do you want to get?" he asks.

I sit back in my chair trying to figure out what to do with my life.

That question is so simple and yet I've never really given it much thought.

Not in any significant way.

It was always so important for me to get good grades and get into the right college and do the right internship and get the best job that I never really stopped to think about whether or not I ever wanted to do that job.

I always defined myself so much in opposition to where I came from that it's difficult to think of myself as someone outside of my past.

Of course, I will never really be free of it, but I am no longer that person either.

Having enough money to live on for a very long time sounds like an ideal situation.

Yet, it brings up other issues, especially for me, someone who doesn't go out much and doesn't really like to party.

What is it that I should do with my life?

"I have no idea," I say, shaking my head.

"What about math? That's what you went to school for."

"And I still like it as a field. But to teach it? Or to write inane test questions that conform to some standard? No, that's not for me."

"You think you'd want to pursue a higher degree in it?" he asks.

I tilt my head back.

That's what I used to want to do.

I got my entry-level job to save up some money and pursue a graduate degree but I never got around to it.

Hmm, that's an idea.

Maybe not a bad one at all.

"What about you?" I ask.

"I have no fucking clue," Owen says after a long pause. "I used to think about all of these things I wanted to do when I was in prison but with a record like mine, there was no way I would ever get hired in any of those fields."

"Well, maybe that's what's really good about what we did. You're someone else now. New name. No record."

"No degree," Owen points out.

"Actually…you're right," I say, raising my eyebrows.

He narrows his eyes trying to read mine.

"Okay, hear me out," I say. "We have money. You have a new name and identity. So, why not enroll in some classes? Why not get a bachelor's degree under your new name?"

"Whaaaat?" Owen says, laughing.

"It's not as ridiculous as it sounds," I say. "I mean, you can study whatever you want and you'll have about four years to figure things out. Besides, then you'll have an actual degree that you've earned."

Owen gets up abruptly and walks over to the kitchen counter.

I wait for him to come back but he doesn't.

After a few moments, I follow him.

His shoulders are tense and moving up and down as he inhales deeply.

I watch for a little bit until I realize what's going on.

He's…crying.

"Owen, are you…" I put my hand on his shoulder.

He turns away from me trying to hide his tears.

"It's okay," I whisper. "It's okay. I'm here."

I wrap my arms around his shoulders and hold him until he stops sobbing.

"I'm sorry about that," he says, pulling away from me. "I'm such a fool."

"No, you're not. But what's going on?"

"I've always wanted to go to college. While I was locked up, that's all I ever thought about. But then I know how much tuition is here and it's not even at the most affordable schools. So I could never justify it."

I shake my head, not understanding what he means.

"Well, what was the point of wasting all of that money on school if I could never use that degree in real life? It was going to be a waste. With my record, I'd never get any job with real prospects. What company would hire me?"

"But that's the thing then, right?" I say, smiling out the corner of my lips.

"Yeah, that's when it first hit me," Owen says. "That's why I got so emotional. Now, with this new identity and the money, I can do whatever I want."

"That's right, you can," I say, patting him on his back.

"Wow," he mumbles to himself, looking down at the floor.

A wave of relief washes over me.

Maybe this is it.

Maybe this is what he needed all along to get that excitement for life back into him.

We collect the dishes and clear the table talking about everything that he could study and everything that he could be.

I am still not sure how it would work if he, for instance, wanted to get a medical degree or anything that required a license, but for now I am just overwhelmed to see him be so happy.

"This is going to be great, Owen. This is going to be so good for you," I say, giving him another hug.

"I think so, too," he says. "Now, how about we celebrate with a bit of ice cream?"

10

OLIVE

WHEN WE CELEBRATE...

Owen is a master at ice cream. To him, it's all about the combination of flavors; a scoop of vanilla with a scoop of caramel, topped with M&Ms and chocolate sauce.

"Are you sure you don't want this?" he asks.

I shake my head.

I'm not eating dairy but I make an exception for tonight and for a little bit of ice cream.

But I draw the line at his concoction.

"I can't believe you're eating all of that," I say.

"It's delicious," he insists.

I put one scoop of chocolate into my bowl and eat a spoonful before sitting down on the couch.

When Owen plops down opposite me, the faux leather couch compresses pushing me upward.

I put my bare feet up on the fluffy ottoman and relish its softness.

I take the remote and start my latest Netflix binge.

We watch for a little while enjoying both our presence and the silence.

I just need to give him more of a chance, I decide. Getting out of prison is a lot like coming back from war, at least according to the articles I read online.

People come out suffering from PTSD and anxiety and they have trouble adjusting to life on the outside.

On top of that, he didn't exactly come out into a stable situation.

Instead of coming home to me, meeting with his parole officer and getting a job, following a curfew and a laid out set of rules, we went on the run.

It probably saved his life but now it's time to do what he was supposed to do.

"How are you feeling?" I ask, turning to him. "About everything?"

"Good. Relieved actually," he says, licking his spoon. "I think I've just been a little lost. And I'm sorry that I have been such an asshole."

I nod.

His apology is nice to hear.

"I was thinking about what we talked about and maybe school is a good option. It will give me a schedule of what to do and some focus. Besides, I really love to learn."

"I know you do," I say, putting my hand on his leg. "It's nice to see this spark again."

"What do you mean?"

"Well, in prison you would always write me about what you'd been reading about and you had all of these ideas about philosophy and life. And when you came out…" My voice trails off.

He waits for me to continue.

"Well, when you came out you seemed to lose that."

Owen hangs his head and buries his fingers in his thick hair.

It has grown a lot since he came out, and he no longer looks so much like a skinhead.

"I was just lost," he says after a moment. "At first, I was just trying to get over the coma and everything that happened—"

"Yes, I'm sure it was so traumatic for you," I say. "Please don't think that I am writing any of that off."

"No, not at all. I'm just trying to explain what's been going on with me."

Now, it's my turn to wait for him to continue.

"I wasn't sure who I was supposed to be out here," he says, exhaling deeply. "After all of those years on the inside, I knew who I was in *there* but out in the free world? I felt like I was walking in a vacuum. Like there was no gravity holding me down. That's probably why so many inmates make bad decisions right after they are released. This feeling of weightlessness is exhilarating at first but then you start to feel sick to your stomach. Nauseous."

I've never thought of it that way.

I mean, I knew that living in prison with all of its rules and regulations would be hard but I didn't quite realize how hard it would be.

"You got some ice cream on your cheek," Owen says, turning toward me.

I wipe something off, but I miss.

He points to his face to show me where it is, but I miss the spot again.

He starts to laugh.

Scooting over, he leans closer to me and runs his thumb gently right below my lower lip.

"Thanks," I say, pulling away but his mouth is suddenly on mine.

He doesn't wait for me to respond before pushing his body against me.

"Wait, what are you doing?" I mumble, trying to push him away.

"I've been waiting to do that for so long, Olive," he mumbles.

It's almost as if he hasn't heard me.

"No, stop," I say louder this time, pushing him away from me as hard as I can.

"What? What's wrong?"

"What are you doing?"

"I love you, Olive."

I get up from the couch and straighten out my clothes.

Those three simple words.

They came out of Owen's mouth so easily.

Why couldn't Nicholas say that?

Why couldn't I say it to him?

"What about that girl you slept with?"

"What about her?"

"I thought you liked her."

"I do. But I love *you*."

"Owen, you're my brother," I say, shaking my head.

"No, I'm not," he says, his voice getting deeper and more forceful. "The sooner you get that through your head the better."

"Don't talk to me like that!" I snap back.

I stand here for a second, at a loss as to what to do.

Then I grab my bowl and bring it to the sink.

I open the faucet to try to tune out this whole thing, both what he did and what he said. But then anger starts to rise up within me.

"Why did you have to do this?" I ask, turning around. "We were having such a nice dinner and everything was good for once."

He glares at me.

"What? Why are you looking at me like that?"

He shakes his head. "Don't you get it? Don't you get that I have been in love with you for a long time?"

"I don't think about you like that, Owen."

"Why not? Because I'm not some con man that lies to you all the time and makes you feel like shit."

"It has nothing to do with Nicholas. You're my brother and nothing is going to change that."

"Oh, yeah?" he says, taking it like a challenge.

Before I realize what's happening, he has me pinned against the wall, pressing his body into mine.

His hands are all over me and down in between my legs.

His tongue is in my mouth.

I try to push him away but he doesn't give me an inch to budge.

"Get off me," I mumble, squeezing my legs shut, but when he presses his forearm against my neck I struggle to breathe.

I gasp for air as my windpipe closes from the pressure.

"How about now? You still think of me as your brother?" he whispers into my ear.

Cold sweat runs down my body.

He releases his hand and I start to cough.

He puts his lips on mine again.

I push him away and this time it works.

He takes a step away from me.

There's a sad puppy expression on his face as if I've done something that hurt him to his core.

"Get the fuck away from me," I say, going to my room.

I throw a few things into a backpack and walk out through the sliding door into the backyard.

I make my way around the pool and go through the side door into the garage for the car.

11

OLIVE

I drive away with tears in my eyes. I feel like such a fool. When I get to the first stop sign, I can barely see and I'm forced to pull over. I cry into the steering wheel.

I blame myself for letting that happen.

I blame myself for trusting him.

I blame myself for believing in him.

But mostly, I mourn what we used to have.

Not long ago, we had the most pure relationship two people could have. We were siblings and we loved each other like siblings.

At least, that's what I thought.

When my tears dry, I look up a hotel or

an Airbnb I can rent in the area. I find another house with a pool for not much more than a hotel room and go with that.

The pool has been one of the most wonderful things about our house and I'm not going to let Owen make me give that up.

Luckily, most of the money is in my account and he doesn't have access to it.

I debate how long I should book this house for, eventually settling on a week. That should give me some time to figure things out.

The check-in instructions arrive via text almost immediately after my payment goes through.

I drive two miles and park the car in front of a little white house with a turquoise door. There's a large gold statue of a greyhound right outside. I run my fingers over its smooth head and snout as I punch the code into the keypad.

There's a wide reclining sectional couch in the middle of the room, facing a huge television. I drop my bag and curl up on it with my phone in my hand. I don't wake up until the sun rises the following morning.

I stretch my arms out and move my neck from side to side. I've never slept in a recliner before but I now know why so many people do. Given everything that happened, my sleep was incredibly restful.

In the kitchen, I make myself some tea and then walk around the house with the cup in my hand.

It's a two-bedroom that looks a lot like the one I rented for Owen and me. Same mid-century modern design with furniture to match. One of the bedrooms leads out to the backyard with a square-shaped pool.

Unable or perhaps unwilling to say no, I strip off my clothes and jump right in.

The water is heated but it's not particularly warm. I dive under and relish in my own weightlessness. My problems start to disappear one by one, as if the water is absorbing them. But that only lasts until I come back to the surface and inhale a breath of air.

Later that morning, I drive by a local juice place and order a green smoothie before heading to a new hiking spot: Tahquitz Canyon.

I've never been there before but reviewers were raving about it on the All Trails app. It's about two miles altogether with a waterfall.

A waterfall in the middle of the desert? This I have to see.

I drive up a steep road going straight into the mountains and park in the lot in front of the visitors' center.

After I pay, I follow the rocky trail further into the valley above the desert floor.

A quarter of the way in, and I'm surrounded by tall granite mountains on three sides.

I scan the sky for possible big horn sheep that the ranger said I might be lucky enough to spot. He has seen groups of them running down the face of one of these mountains at full speed. A mountain lion, who's about seven feet in length and two hundred pounds, is known to wander these parts and the ranger suspected that he was the one chasing them.

I'm in awe at how close nature and civilization exist out in the west. At night, I hear coyotes howling and here, only a few miles away from my house, there are mountain lions and big horn sheep living their lives. Some people might be put off by that, but I love it.

I've lived in a city for a very long time and only now realize how claustrophobic it can be.

There is a disconnect between the urban me and the wild me.

Out here, I take a breath of fresh air and I feel free.

Freer than I ever felt back east.

The trail continues to get steeper and steeper and I'm forced to take a few short rests after I start to feel dizzy.

If you keep doing this long enough, you'll get stronger, I say to myself. Take a minute to stop to rest but keep going.

It's going to be worth it in the end.

I start up the audiobook again. This isn't my usual reading but I saw it and bought it on impulse.

It's about a woman who hiked the

Pacific Crest Trail from Mexico to Canada. The hike is over twenty-five hundred miles and takes about six months or so.

Today, I'm struggling with doing only two.

When I reach the middle of the hike, I can't believe my eyes. In the middle of one of the harshest and hottest deserts in the world, there's a tall waterfall.

All of the falling water has formed a crystal clear lake in front of it.

It's a weekday and I'm the only one here.

I take off my shoes and wade in. The water is much colder than in my pool but still warm enough to enjoy. In the blistering heat that made me sweat completely through my shirt, it's actually quite refreshing.

I love taking pictures and I even brought a selfie stick with me.

I take pictures of the shore from inside the lake and of myself with the water all of the way up to my shoulders.

Somewhat near the waterfall, there's a

towering boulder about twenty feet tall that's shaped like an egg.

The valley curves around it, but there's still space in between the wall and the boulder to get through on the other side.

Suddenly, I regret the fact that I brought my phone.

I wade back to shore, drop it off, and rush back over. The only way to get closer to the waterfall is to swim or to press your back against the boulder and your feet against the granite wall and scoot through the opening.

I figure I'll try the latter first and then if I fall in, I'll just swim.

A little bit into the process, I suddenly start to freak out.

There is no one around and I worry about falling in and hitting my head.

I should've just started swimming.

Why am I being so stupid?

These thoughts start to crowd out my judgement and a panicky feeling rises through my body.

I take a few deep breaths to calm myself. Then I talk to myself out loud.

"It's going to be okay, everything is fine. If you want to swim, just swim. Let go of your feet and slowly fall in. You won't hit your head."

My body doesn't comply.

Instead, I continue to move slowly wedged in between two boulders until I climb out on the other side.

I let out a deep sigh of relief.

The waterfall isn't big and it's an easy swim under it.

But I just sit on the ledge on the other side of the boulder and look up.

Through the sunshine and against the bright blue sky, the falling water looks like it's peppered with a thousand different diamonds.

Mesmerized, I wrap my hands around my knees and lose myself in the beauty.

I stay by the waterfall for a long time enjoying the solitude and the silence until a group of loud rowdy fifty year olds show up.

They talk and laugh loudly, breaking my trance.

When I get back to shore, one of the

men makes a joke about how he'd go skinny dipping but only if I do.

How dare you pollute this beautiful spot with your unwanted sexual come-ons? I want to ask him, but I don't say anything.

I ball up my fists instead and wait for the desire to punch him to wear off.

When I get back to my car, I make a decision. I'm going to find my mother.

12

OLIVE

WHEN I GO TO FIND HER...

W hen I put her address into Google Maps on my phone, my hands start to tremble.

I've looked it up before, but I've never done it with the intention of actually going there.

Now that it's time, I feel sick to my stomach.

A million what-if possibilities run through my mind.

What if she doesn't want to see me?

What if she slams the door in my face?

What if she says that she doesn't know what I'm talking about?

I'd spend the rest of the day reading

stories about adopted children finding their parents.

In some cases, they are happy to see them but in most they aren't. Maybe it's just this website's bias (the people who are using it to vent about their problems) but I try to prepare myself for the worst case scenario. She could say that I'm mistaken and that she wants me to leave her property.

Air bursts out of me before I even realize that I've been holding my breath.

"Okay, stop catastrophizing. Just drive," I say to myself out loud.

I turn onto a road going up into the mountains, first winding its way past a mobile home community.

I glance at the phone.

Her house is still a little bit further. When I drive a little too slow, the car behind me beeps. There isn't anywhere to pull over to let them through so I speed up.

Just around another bend is where the mansions start. I saw this when I looked at her house on my computer last night.

The car behind me turns into one gate and I continue further.

Three more houses later, and I turn into her driveway.

There's an intercom next to a beautiful modern oak gate. I'm too far away from it to reach it from my car, so I'm forced to put it in park and climb out.

I look at the buttons.

Despite how much I've examined this house from satellite, somehow I haven't considered the fact that I could be turned away even before I actually get to see her.

My heart starts to beat erratically.

If whoever answers isn't her and they don't let me in, what do I do then?

I tap my fingers on my thigh. Then without pressing any buttons, I get back inside and close the door.

I don't know what to say and I can't press that button until I do.

I sit in the car for some time trying to figure everything out.

For some reason, it never occurred to me that I wouldn't see her open the door.

Why not? I had so much time to think everything through.

I thought that I would at least have that even if the entire conversation went to shit.

And now?

What if someone else answers the door?

What do I say to them?

A loud beep startles me.

"Can I help you?" someone asks.

I stare at the intercom through my open window, unable to move an inch.

"Excuse me? Can you hear me?"

The voice belongs to a woman but I can't tell how old she is.

"Um, yes…I'm here to see Josephine Rose Reyes," I say slowly.

There's a silence on the other end.

"Or maybe Josephine Rose Lebold now?"

"Who is this?"

"I'm…" I start to say but then I stop.

I don't know who I'm talking to.

It might be a housekeeper or a sister or a daughter.

I don't know how much anyone in her family knows about me and I don't want to make a relationship between us more difficult to establish.

"It's personal. I'm just looking for her. Does she live here?"

"Please tell me your name," the voice says after a long exhalation.

I take a deep breath.

"I'm not going to let you in here without your name," the woman says.

Now, it's my turn to exhale.

"My name is Olive Kernes."

"Hold on a minute," she says.

A long pause follows and then another.

When I'm about to give up on her, the gate starts to slide open.

I drive up the long driveway leading up to a very modern glass house overlooking a cliff.

I park my car in the driveway and walk up the steps lined by orange trees on both sides.

There is a large double door made of distressed wood the color of caramel. One of them has a wrought iron door knocker.

I'm about to use it when the lock spins.

"That's simply for decorative purposes," a woman with her hair in a bun says.

With pursed lips, lined a nude color, a knee-length black dress, and a pristine white apron on top of it, she looks like a housekeeper in the movies.

I had no idea anyone really employed people who looked like this.

"Hi, I'm Olive Kernes," I introduce myself, extending my hand.

She shakes my hand but I can tell that my gesture throws her off.

It's like she never expected me to introduce myself to her.

"Please follow me," the housekeeper says, without giving me her name in response.

I walk through an enormous marble archway and into an equally spacious living room that's surrounded completely by glass. The views of the valley are expansive and magnificent.

"This way please, ma'am," the housekeeper says.

I follow her down a large white hallway into another portion of the house.

This looks like something of a sitting room. There are two luxurious couches facing one another and pointed at a large fireplace.

A beautiful wingback chair sits at the head and a large marble coffee table centers the entire room. I look around for a television but I don't find one.

"Please wait here while I get Mrs. Jemisin."

The view pulls on me as if it were a gravitational force.

The windows start at the floor and span the whole length of the wall, all twelve or so feet, up to the ceiling.

Instead of sliding open, they fold open like an accordion but their hinges are so thin they are practically invisible.

"Olive," someone calls my name.

Her voice is quiet and delicate and I stand here for a moment without turning to face her to relish the moment.

13

OLIVE

WHEN I SEE HER...

"Olive," she says again.

I take a deep breath, gather my courage, and turn around.

The woman before me is about average height but petite in frame. She is in her early forties but she could easily pass for thirty-five.

Dressed in leggings and a loose t-shirt, she doesn't look like someone who would own a house like this.

"You're….Josephine," I say quietly.

She gives me a slight nod and asks me to sit down.

It's only now that I notice that she's not wearing shoes or socks and has a silver anklet with a palm tree around her right foot.

She takes a seat in the wingback chair and crosses her legs.

"How can I help you?" she asks.

Either she has no idea why I'm really here or she is playing her cards close to her chest.

I sit on the edge of the couch next to her and take a deep breath.

Afraid to meet her eyes, I look a little past her.

How did I not notice this before? The wall is covered with pictures of her family.

There are photos of Josephine and her husband in cities all over the world. Intermixed with shots of them in London, Rome, and Sydney are pictures of them near waterfalls and glaciers.

"Is that your family?" I ask, pointing to the picture closest to her.

It's her smiling ear to ear with her husband and two small kids, both under the age of five.

"Yes," she says softly.

I wait for her to elaborate but she doesn't. "How can I help you, Olive?"

Right, of course.

She wants to get to the point.

I'm stalling.

Not just because I'm afraid to come right out and say what I need to say but also because I want to spend as much time with her as possible before she kicks me out.

"What does your husband do?" I blurt out.

The question is about as inappropriate as one could be, but once it's out there I can't really take it back.

"He works for me," she says, broadening her shoulders and smiling out of the corners of her lips. "With me," she adds.

"Oh, I'm so sorry," I add, totally humiliated.

Why did I just assume that she had all of this because of a man?

And even if I did, why did I come right out and say it?

I'm such an idiot.

"What can I help you with, Olive?" Josephine asks, pushing back her long sandy hair from one shoulder to another.

I take a deep breath.

When I open my mouth, it goes completely dry.

I start to say something but then I can't help but cough. Not wanting her to think that I'm stonewalling, I start anyway.

"I'm your daughter," I say, clearing my throat.

The housekeeper placed two glasses of water on the coffee table before she left and I take a sip of mine.

Josephine doesn't react.

I expect her to either be happy or mad but she has absolutely no reaction. Her effect remains flat and I'm not sure what to do with that.

"Um, I got your records from a private investigator and it seems to all check out."

"Can I see them please?" she asks.

I reach into my backpack and pull out the folder with all of the information that I have on her.

It's only when she has it in her hands

that I realize that I should've probably
made a copy of this.

What if she takes them?

What I lose the only information that I
have? The only proof!

I scoot to the edge of the couch and sit
as close to her as possible as she lays the
folder on her lap.

She goes through it, examining each
page carefully.

Then she reaches the results of the
DNA test.

"How did they get these DNA results?"
she asks.

"I'm not sure. He worked for my ex-
boyfriend, I never met him. But I think
he probably followed you and took it off a
cup of coffee you discarded, or something
like that."

Josephine closes the folder slowly and
looks up at me. It's only when our eyes
meet that I see the tears in hers.

"Olive," she says quietly, pressing her
index finger into her eye to make it stop. "I
am your mother."

I sit here, dumbfounded, until she

throws her arms around me. "I've been looking for you for…so long," she whispers into my ear.

Tears start to well up and stream down my face.

I wipe them off but more come.

After a few moments, I give up and just let myself cry.

We hold each other for some time before we finally pull away. This is so beyond the response that I thought I would get.

At first, she seemed quiet, cold even, but now I realize she just wanted to make sure that I was really who I was saying I was before confirming.

"Tell me about yourself," Josephine says. "Tell me everything."

I don't know where to start but I take a deep breath and just begin.

I tell her about how I grew up and about my family. I gloss over the addiction and my brother being in prison.

We have just met and I don't want to dump all the shit from my life directly in her lap.

I'm not family, so I focus on myself. I tell her about all of the studying that I did in high school and Wellesley College.

"Oh my God, you went to Wellesley!" she shrieks. "Wow, that's such a great school."

"I'm so relieved you've heard of it," I say. "You'd be surprised how many haven't."

"It's one of the best liberal colleges around. It's steeped in history. I'm so proud of you!"

I give her a small smile but then my lips part on their own and I grin from ear to ear.

I don't know how long I have wanted my mother to say that to me.

More tears start to collect. I sniff my nose to try to make them go away.

"What's wrong? What did I say?" she asks, draping her arm around my shoulder.

"I'm just so…relieved that you are happy to see me," I mumble. "I wasn't sure how you would react with just some stranger coming into your life completely unannounced."

She gives me a squeeze and a peck on the cheek.

I want to ask her what happened and why she gave me up but I want to know more about her first.

"Did you go to college?" I ask.

She nods.

"After I moved out here to California, I went to Santa Monica College, which is a community college, and then I transferred to USC. That's where I graduated from."

"Wow, University of Southern California. That's a pretty big deal."

"I liked it a lot. That's where my husband and I met."

She points to the picture on the wall. I look at him more carefully.

He has trustworthy eyebrows and a strong Roman nose.

"So, you have been together ever since?" I ask.

"We've been together since my second semester there, since I was twenty," she says.

Suddenly, a gulf forms in between everything that we should be talking about and what we are actually talking about.

I try to keep the conversation going on this level but I simply can't.

I look up at her and see her watching me.

"Why don't you ask me what you came here to ask me?" Josephine says quietly.

14

OLIVE

WHEN I ASK HER...

I sit back into the couch, trying to make myself as small as possible. I want to know, of course, but I don't want to ask.

I don't want this beautiful moment between us to dissipate.

"Why did you give me up?" I ask, swallowing hard.

"I didn't," she says quietly.

Then she moves to the edge of her chair and puts her hands on my knee. "You have to believe me, Olive. You were the only thing I wanted and what happened to you wasn't up to me."

I don't know how to process this. My

fingers go numb and my stomach starts to do somersaults.

"What do you mean?" I manage to ask.

"Your father and I were deeply in love," she says, biting her lower lip as if thinking about him still gives her pain to this very day. "My parents didn't approve. His mother didn't either. We were rich. He was poor. According to my father, he didn't belong in our prep school even though he was probably the smartest kid there."

I nod.

"His name was Danny Lebold."

From the folder, I knew his name but not anything else about him except that she took his name at one point.

Wait, a second.

She used past tense.

I look up at her trying not to let my mind go there.

"Danny died in a car accident," she says slowly. "The night that we were supposed to run away together. I waited for him and he never showed up. I later learned that his car got pushed out into traffic by another car and someone going sixty miles an hour ran into his driver's door, killing him instantly."

I put my hand over my mouth and shake my head.

"Everyone said it was an accident but I didn't believe it. Not then, not now."

"What do you think happened?"

"I think my father organized the whole thing. I don't have any proof but he would do anything to stop us."

"You really think he did that?" I ask, trying to figure out if she actually just told me that my grandfather put a hit out on my father.

"I had my doubts before but after I ran away to California by myself to keep you safe, they found me. I started having contractions and I checked into a hospital. They had their investigative team all around the country working on it and they found me."

She stops talking for a moment, trying to collect her thoughts. I want to urge her to keep talking but I give her some time.

"The labor wasn't going well. It was

taking forever and at some point my blood pressure started to drop and they wheeled me into a room for an emergency c-section."

I nod.

"Unlike a planned one, for an emergency c-section, they knock you out completely," she adds.

I nod again.

She looks up at me with tears in her eyes. She doesn't wipe them away this time. Instead, she just stares at me and touches my cheek with her warm palm.

"When I woke up, they told me you had died," she says.

Cold shivers run down my spine.

"What do you mean?"

She shrugs. "They told me you had died but they wouldn't show me the body. Then my parents came in and my mom told me not to worry and how sorry she was about everything. No one would answer any of my questions. I even called the police but the doctor and my parents talked to them and I was underage, and somehow this whole thing got swept under the table. They told them that I was just upset about the stillbirth."

"Oh my God," I whisper.

"I tried to look for you but my parents were this vault. I couldn't get anything out of them. Stillbirths don't really get funerals, at least my parents refused to put one together. They just forced me to go back home with them and never talk about it again."

"Is that what you did?"

"Briefly." She nods. "I was so exhausted from the birth both mentally and physically, and then I was so overwhelmed by everything that happened afterward. I didn't know what to do. I didn't know what happened to you. I didn't want to believe that you had died but I had no proof. I felt like I was going crazy."

I shake my head again, trying to internalize everything that she's saying.

"I came back to California about three months later. I ran away again, only this time I took all of my money and I stayed quiet until I turned eighteen. Then there was nothing they could do to bring me back."

"So…how did you find out about me?" I ask.

"I started school. I got a job at a library. I tried to move on with my life but I couldn't let it go. I ended up hiring a private investigator but after months of looking, he didn't find a thing. What he did confirm, however, was that you were never a stillbirth and that was *something*, at least."

She gets up from her seat and walks around the room, looking at the pictures on the wall. There's a vase full of daisies that she adjusts slightly by moving a few stems around.

"When my mom got sick, she passed really quickly," Josephine says. "And a few days before, I was with her and she was on a lot of medication and I just asked about you. She apologized and said you never died. That my father had arranged for you to be adopted by some family up north. They weren't wealthy so they were very much 'motivated by money' - his words. And as long as the money continued to come, they'd never tell you the truth."

I put my head in between my legs and take a few deep breaths. My heart feels like it's beating out of my chest.

"Are you okay?" Josephine rushes over to me.

"Yes, I'm fine," I say looking up at her. "I just got a bit…overwhelmed."

"My mom had a picture of you that one of the intermediaries involved with this so-called adoption had sent her," Josephine says after a moment. "You were five and you look exactly like you do now. Grown up, of course, but you're a carbon copy of that little girl."

She pulls the picture out of the top drawer of the dresser. It's inside a book of Emily Dickinson poems.

I look at it. I've never seen it before but I'm dressed in my favorite green dress and I'm smiling from ear to ear.

"I knew who you were the minute you walked into the house," Josephine admits. "I just couldn't believe my eyes. And when I saw the results of that DNA test… I don't know why I needed to see them after all of this time but I guess it had something to do with all of the lies that I've been fed by my family."

"I'm so sorry," I whisper.

"You have nothing to be sorry for," she says, hugging me and pulling me close to her. "I'm the one who is sorry. I am so sorry that I wasn't there for you all of these years."

We sob in each other's arms for a long time.

After I dry my tears, something occurs to me.

"Why didn't you find me after you learned that I wasn't dead?" I ask.

15

OLIVE

WHEN I DON'T HEAR FROM HER...

A t first, the silence is deafening. She sits back in her chair and crosses her legs. I sit back as well and brace myself for the answer.

If she found out about me when I was five, why didn't she try to find me again?

What could've stopped her from looking for me?

"I only found out about you a year ago," Josephine says, the pupils in her almond eyes dilating.

"What?" I gasp.

"My mother held onto that picture all of those years but she never showed it to me. I had no idea who you lived with. I didn't even know your name."

I cover my mouth with my hand and shake my head.

I try to imagine how painful this must have been for her, but all I can think of is my own pain.

My heart tightens and pounds so loudly that I think it's going to burst out of my chest.

"I hired another private investigator to try to find you but I didn't know much. I didn't know your name or where you lived. My father refused to talk about any of it. He still insists that you were a stillborn. All the PI had was this picture and it wasn't much."

We hold each other for a while after that.

When she pulls away, I don't want to let go out of fear that I'm going to lose her again.

She asks me more about how my private investigator found out about her, but I don't know any of the details.

I told her that the man I dated at the

time had a lot of connections and he worked for him.

"Well, he did one hell of a job," she says.

Suddenly, my body begins to shake.

"What? What's wrong?" Josephine puts her arm around me.

"I'm so, so sorry," I whisper. "I was just so worried about coming here. I thought I was going to have a panic attack. I thought that for sure you were going to slam the door in my face."

"No," she says categorically. "No, I would never do that."

"I know, now," I say with a whimper.

I give her another hug and ask if we can talk about something else. A big smile comes over her face.

I spend a few more hours there, taking turns telling her about my life and listening to hers.

Not wanting to overstay my welcome, I tell her that I have to go.

I don't want to.

I want to stay and spend as much time

with her as possible but I want to pace myself.

I don't want to be one of those annoying guests that is fun to spend time with at first but who never knows when to leave.

I make a general suggestion that we should get together again this week, and she surprises me by asking if I want to have lunch tomorrow.

Driving back home, I feel almost lethargic.

All of the anticipation and anxiety has put a big stress on my adrenal system and now that the moment has passed all I want to do is sleep forever. When I get back to the Airbnb, I head straight to the bedroom and curl up under the covers.

I review everything that's happened over and over again, somewhat unable to believe my own experience.

I thought that she would take her time accepting me.

I thought she would be more suspicious.

I'd prepared myself for that because

that's what all of the online forums said,
no matter how much you may want to just
run into her arms, she's a stranger who
feels bad about what she has done and you
want to respect her boundaries.

***

THE FOLLOWING DAY, THINGS SHIFT.

Josephine calls and says that something
has come up and she has to reschedule.

"I'm free tomorrow," I say a little bit
too eagerly.

"No, actually tomorrow won't work
either. I have a lot of work to catch up on.
I'll get back to you in a few days. Hope
that's okay."

There isn't much more to the
conversation than that. I stare at the
phone for a very long time after she
hangs up. What did I do? What just
happened?

The following few days pass in a daze.
I don't have the energy to do much so I
just stay at home reading, watching
television, and looking through old

magazines that the owners have laying around.

As much as I try to put it out of my mind, my thoughts keep circling back to Josephine.

Did something happen after I left? Was she just being nice when I came over? Did I imagine the whole interaction altogether?

Five days later, my phone rings while I am swimming in the pool. Enough time has passed that I'm no longer rushing to it to answer it.

The only person who has called me this whole time was Owen and I have no intentions of talking to him.

When I get out and dry myself off, I look down at the screen. It's Josephine. She doesn't leave a message but a text arrives a moment later.

Sorry I've been MIA this week. Had to catch up on a lot of work. You want to get some lunch?

I stare at the phone reading the words over and over again. Did she really send this?

Sure, where? When? I text back.

An hour later, we meet on the main

drag of Palm Canyon Drive at a place called Tac/Quila, a modern Mexican restaurant. Much to my surprise, I am not particularly nervous to see her again.

I probably would have been if we had met up a few days ago like we had planned but after all of this time, I am just annoyed. I don't want it to show so I keep my feelings bottled up and put a smile on my face as I follow the hostess to her table.

Josephine sits leaning over the menu to a vertical garden that spans the entire wall behind her.

"Wow, what a beautiful spot," I say when we embrace.

"It's so good to see you," Josephine says. "I am so sorry for cancelling before but I just had so much work to catch up on."

I nod and give her a slight smile. Suddenly, I realize that I don't even know what she does for a living.

When we order drinks, I ask her about it.

"Oh, you don't know who I am?" she asks, raising her eyebrows.

She puts her elbow on the edge of the table and plays with the back of her hair for a moment.

"Should I?" I ask, tilting my head to one side.

"Well, no, I'm not *that* famous. But I just thought you knew because you knew about me."

16

OLIVE

I'd gone through the contents of the folder that I had received but none of the information had anything about what she did for work.

"I'm a writer," she says, smiling. "I don't know if you like to read or not, but I write romantic suspense novels."

"Really?!" I ask, leaning closer to her. "I love to read. Romance and thrillers are my favorite."

"Good." She smiles. "Me, too."

"But I never saw your name anywhere. Oh, I guess you don't write under Josephine Jemisin though."

"No, I actually write under a completely different name. Lauren Hart."

My mouth drops open.

My ears start to buzz.

"No," I say with disbelief. "No, you're not her!"

Josephine laughs, tilting her head back.

"I love Lauren Hart! She's one of my favorite writers. I read everything she writes."

I don't know why I keep talking about her as if she's not her except that I am still having trouble processing this revelation.

It's hard to put into words exactly how much I love Lauren Hart's writing.

She writes in first person and you get this sense that you are going through whatever the character is going through. Plus, she captures details unlike anyone else I've ever read.

Our drinks arrive. I take a sip of mine.

"I'm so sorry," I say, looking down at the table. "You're just one of my favorite writers and I had no idea that you are... her and she is you."

"It's okay," she says, putting her hand

on mine. "It's really sweet actually. I love hearing from my readers and I had no idea that my long lost daughter was one of them."

She looks away for a moment and then back at me.

I can see that she's trying to push away a tear. She bites her lower lip and picks up the drink that was just delivered.

"I want to make a toast," she says. "I have been looking for you for a very long time, Olive. I've loved you ever since I found out that I was pregnant and I never stopped. Everyone told me that you were dead but I never stopped believing."

Tears are flowing down her face freely now.

She doesn't try to hide them or to stop them.

"I want to drink to you and to thank you for coming here and finding me," she says. I start to sob along with her.

"Thank you," I mumble through my tears, wiping off my cheeks. "Thank you for welcoming me and for accepting me."

We clink our glasses.

The glass feels cool against my hot lips and the cocktail tastes like heaven.

"Wow, this is amazing," I say, pulling it away from my mouth.

"I know, they make the best drinks here. And the food is to die for as well," Josephine says. "What did you get?"

"The refrescado," I say.

I look down at the menu and read the ingredients: blanco tequila, agave, lime and lemon juice, and cucumber water.

"It's like cucumber water but so much more," I add. "It's so refreshing."

"Mine's really good, too."

She gives it to me to try and I take a few sips.

Suddenly, we are no longer strangers. We are almost like long lost friends or, dare I say, family.

Over lunch, she tells me all about how she always loved to read and has wanted to be a writer ever since she was a little girl.

After majoring in English at USC, she went on to get a graduate degree there along with a PhD but after graduation she knew for sure that she didn't want to work in education.

She started out like many others, writing short stories and submitting them to literary magazines.

"The ability to handle rejection is one of those things you really need to develop as a writer if you want to pursue traditional publishing," she says when our fried avocado bites arrive. "When I wrote my first novel, a young adult paranormal romance about a werewolf, I sent it out to about forty different agents. Most didn't write back but the few that did sent back form rejection letters."

"Wow, I had no idea that it was so brutal," I say.

"It's kind of like acting. You just have to brace yourself for rejection and not take it personally. Otherwise, it's never going to work out."

"So, what happened then?" I ask.

"I wrote more. I wrote a sci-fi dystopian novel with my husband. We alternated writing different chapters. While he worked, I traveled to Texas to a writers' conference to pitch the book to agents."

"And that worked?" I ask her eagerly.

"I was scared shitless to present the pitch. I'm not much of a public speaker. But I did it and they both asked me to send it to them. Well, I was really excited and that's what I planned on doing. The conference itself had a lot of different seminars so I attended as many as I could. One of the ones that I went to at the very end was this one that Deanna Roy ran.

"It was all about romance writing and how she quit her job as a teacher because she was able to make about thirty grand a year as an independent author. Well, I had no knowledge about this whole field up until that point. I mean, I knew that romance existed but I'd never read any modern indie romance books."

She stops talking to dunk the last avocado bite into their magnificent spicy sauce.

"What happened then?" I ask.

"I took lots of notes and when I went home, I got to work. I started researching as much as I could about the industry. I read a lot of books, I realized that I could totally write this kind of book, and I dove right in. There were a lot of other things involved in the process as well. I had to learn a lot about marketing and advertising and things like that, but it started to work. When I got started, I thought just like that author. I was like, if I could just make thirty grand a year doing what I love, that would be enough to keep going."

"And now…you have that huge house!" I say.

I immediately want to take it back because of how crude it comes out but she laughs.

"My husband quit his job and he does a lot of the financial parts of the business. But yes, after a lot of books and a lot of hard work, we were able to buy that amazing house."

"Your parents must be so proud," I say.

"I don't talk to them. I haven't talked to them for many years after your birth and I only briefly reconnected with my mother before her death. They aren't part of my life and I will never take a penny from them. My siblings can have all of that."

17

OLIVE

WHEN I REALIZE THAT I'M A BAD FRIEND...

Josephine and I talk a lot about school and how much we both enjoy learning.

I tell her about majoring in mathematics and how much I enjoyed the subject in school but not once I got out into the real world.

I tell her the truth about everything except for what happened over the last year of my life.

I don't know her well and I don't trust myself to dump everything that has happened with Nicholas and Owen into her lap. I'm afraid the drama would make her run away from me.

Instead, I just tell her the basics.

I tell her about Owen and his past. I tell her that I dated someone named Nicholas but we broke up. I tell her that my ex-boyfriend's private investigator found her information and I wanted to come here and take a little break from work and find her.

When she asks how long I'm staying, I say at least for a few more weeks.

The word 'ex-boyfriend' still hurts when I say it out loud.

It feels like he has barely been my boyfriend and now he's already an ex that I'm supposed to get over. When I share this with Josephine, she says that it's important to take some time to focus on myself, otherwise my baggage from my old relationship will leak over into my new one.

A new relationship? Wow, what a novel idea.

Of course, it's possible, and likely, but somehow even trying to imagine myself with someone who is not Nicholas makes me feel strange.

THE FOLLOWING DAY, I FACETIME WITH Sydney and I tell her everything.

When I take a brief pause, she asks why she had cancelled our plans to meet up the next day.

"Apparently, she had to work," I say. "She has a tight deadline to get her new novel written and she didn't want to meet up for lunch in the middle of her writing days. She said that she raced through that book in order to get it done as quickly as possible and meet up with me."

"I'm really happy for you," Sydney says, turning her face away from the camera. I give her a second but then move my face a little bit closer.

What is going on here? Is she….upset?

"Syd, are you okay?" I ask.

"Yes, I'm fine," she whispers and her voice cracks in the middle.

"What's wrong?"

"Nothing," she says, shaking her head. "I'm so stupid. I can't stop this."

When she looks up at me, I see tears streaming down her face.

"Oh my God, what's going on?" I demand to know.

"James and I broke up," she says quickly, jumping over each word. "I'm so sorry. I didn't want to bring this up. You're in such a good mood with everything that has happened—"

"Forget all that. Tell me what's going on," I insist, feeling like the most egocentric idiot.

How could I just go on like that?

How could I not notice that something was wrong?

Here she is going through something traumatic and I'm just going on about how wonderful my life is. I want to be able to rewind our whole conversation and start again.

Sydney doesn't reply and just continues to nudge me to keep talking. But I refuse.

"Please, you have to tell me. Everything is fine with me. I've already talked enough."

"Okay," she says, taking a deep breath.

And then she takes another one.

And another one.

"I caught him cheating on me," she says, shaking her head.

I narrow my eyes.

"I know, I know, it's so stupid. I mean, he can't cheat on me, right? We've been together with other people, so what am I complaining about?"

"That's not what I think," I say sternly. "And you know that."

She shrugs. "That's what I think. That's what he thinks."

I wait for her to explain. It takes a bit more coaxing but eventually she does.

"I came home early from work one day and found him in bed with his ex-girlfriend."

"But doesn't she live in…Hawaii?"

"She lives in California. He moved to Hawaii after they broke up. When I looked through his phone later, I discovered that they'd started messaging each other long before we even met. They were friendly at first, but soon it got sexual. She had a fiancé. He kept wanting her to break things off with him. But she didn't. She married him. But they continued texting and talking and sending each other videos and naked pictures."

"I'm so, so sorry," I whisper, wishing more than anything that I was right there with her so that I could take her into my arms.

"It's so stupid. I'm so stupid. This has been going on this whole time and I didn't see it."

"He was probably very good at hiding it."

"He was," she admits. "All of her conversations and videos were in a special folder. He only showed it to me after we argued for hours and I basically told him I was leaving."

"So, she flew out there to be with him?" I ask, trying to figure out the details of the story.

Sydney nods her head and buries it in her hands again.

For a moment, all I see is an extreme close up of her forehead. Her sobs reverberate around the whole living room.

"She was in New York on business so she came to visit him in our apartment. Our bed. When I finally got him to admit the truth, he said that she has been there the whole week. Staying with him during the days while I was at work."

"What an asshole," I say under my breath.

"You've got that right."

"So…what happened?"

"What do you think? I yelled. She put her clothes on and left. We yelled some more. Then we talked. Then I cried. Then I told him I never wanted to see him again."

I guess that's about it. That's pretty much the anatomy of a breakup.

She lets out a big sigh and buries her head in her hands.

"Will you stay with me here for a while?" Sydney asks.

"Yes, we can talk for as long as you want."

"No, I don't want to talk. Let's do something else. How about watch Netflix?"

"Sure. What do you have in mind?"

"Something dark and painful. Something we've seen before."

I know what she's going to suggest even before she says it. I put it on my TV and she starts it up on hers. When the opening credits start and sync up, we both start to laugh a little.

"There's nothing like watching someone else go through hell when things get shitty in your life, huh?" I ask.

She nods and we start to watch the first episode.

18

OLIVE

I haven't seen Owen in almost ten days. I rented the Airbnb for just one week initially but then extended it to another two.

I still haven't made up my mind as to what to do about him.

Mainly, I haven't wanted to deal with him at all so I've just been ignoring his calls.

Today is no different.

I don't want to see him, and I don't want to talk about anything that happened that night.

I don't know how far he would've taken it if I hadn't physically stopped him, but he was certainly not taking no for an answer.

I shake my head as anger starts to well up within me thinking back to that night.

How dare he? Who does he think he is? What right did he think he had to do anything like that?

I pull up a little bit down the street and walk over.

The front door is probably locked and I have no intention of using it in any case so I jump the fence in the back.

There are no windows in the garage so I have no way of knowing if his car is there or not.

I did peek through the windows of the living room when I walked by but didn't see anyone there.

His room faces the neighbor's yard so there's no real way of knowing if he's home or not.

Instead of being drenched in sweat and with my heart pounding in my chest, I feel calm and collected.

My hands aren't even shaking.

When I reach the sliding door of my old bedroom, I let out a sigh of relief.

Yes! The door is open.

I left it this way but there was a big possibility that he would've locked it afterward.

It slides open smoothly and I walk onto the carpet.

I tried to pack everything that was important to me when I took off, but I forgot this.

It's a small silver necklace of a tree of life that Nicholas gave me. I looked around for it everywhere and then remembered that I had placed it inside the vanity of the master bathroom. It wasn't with the rest of my jewelry and I couldn't let it stay here much longer.

I don't know what Owen's plans are but I needed to get this back. It's not worth much but Nicholas bought it for me just because and I love it.

I tiptoe to the bathroom and open the mirror, holding my breath.

I find it right where I left it and I drop it into my pocket.

"What are you doing here?" His voice startles me.

I flip around with my back against the faucet.

"I forgot something," I say, standing upright and trying to look as big as possible.

The room is big for a bathroom, but it feels small.

The more seconds tick by the more the walls feel like they are closing in around me.

"Where have you been?" Owen asks.

His voice is deep but not slurred.

He looks tired and worn out, like he hasn't slept for days.

His skin is sallow, gray even. There are big black circles under his eyes.

"I rented another place," I say. "I needed some space."

"Are you ever coming back?"

"No," I say. I'm tempted to add, "I don't think so," but I don't.

I don't want to give him anymore hope than absolutely necessary.

I am not coming back here and I'm not going to live with him.

"Are you back with Nicholas?" he asks.

I furrow my brow. Where is this coming from?

"No, of course not. Nicholas is gone. I have no idea where he is."

"Yeah, right," he says under his breath.

I don't care that he doesn't believe me. I'm tired of having this fight over and over again.

"So, what have you been doing there at your new place?" Owen asks, leaning against the doorframe, physically creating a barrier between me and the exit.

"I don't know. Hiking, swimming, reading. What have you been doing?" I leave the topic of my mother out on purpose.

"Drinking," he says, laughing.

"Are you sure that's such a good idea?"

"No, of course not. But who says that living is such a good idea?"

I shake my head.

I don't know what else I can do for him.

I try to get past him but he stops me.

He puts his arm out, blocking the door.

"I'm leaving," I say, pushing past him.

"I'm sorry, okay!" he yells after me. "I'm sorry I did that, but I love you."

I don't turn around.

He wants me to engage and that's the last thing I want.

I head down the long hallway and turn left where it splits off. The kitchen is to the right and the front door is to the left.

"I love you!" Owen yells after me. "Why won't you believe me?"

"I do believe you but I don't love you back," I say, grabbing the door handle.

As soon as I turn it, Owen pounces over and pushes it shut.

We are face-to-face.

We're so close I can feel his breath on me.

"You just don't want to move in because you're going to see Nicholas again, huh?" he asks.

His eyes are wild and out of control.

"I don't know why you're obsessed with him. We're not together anymore."

"You miss him," Owen says in an accusatory tone.

"Of course, I miss him. I thought we would be together forever. So what? Life happens, right?"

I take a few steps away from him into the living room, hoping that he will follow me there.

That way, once he is distracted, I can slip out of the front door.

"Nicholas is a murderer," Owen says, pacing around the living room.

Suddenly, it occurs to me that he is not just drunk. He is also intoxicated on something else.

Something not at all mellow like pot, something potent.

I'm tempted to ask but I don't want to make him even more agitated.

This is why I left. I'm not going to tiptoe around my own house out of fear of making someone upset by my presence.

"I'm tired of talking about him," I say, folding my arms across my chest. "We're no longer together, what more do you want?"

"I want you to believe that he killed my girlfriend and his partner. The FBI is looking for him. What more proof do you need?"

"I'm going to believe what I want to believe, Owen. You're not going to tell me what to think."

A part of me is proud of myself for standing my ground, but another part is terrified.

He already attacked me once.

He tried to keep me cloistered in the bathroom.

What's to stop him from doing it again? One false move on my part and he will.

He looks down at the floor and hangs his shoulders.

He's giving up. I see that as my moment.

"I'm going to go now, Owen," I say and move slowly toward the door.

It was a toss-up whether I should've just slipped out or whether it was better to warn him that I was leaving and I chose the latter.

When I open the door, I turn back once and see that Owen has sat down in the large chair opposite the couch.

I let out a small sigh of relief.

Then he starts to laugh. I'm about to close the door but curiosity stops me in my tracks.

"What's so funny?" I ask, peeking my head back in.

He continues to chuckle, raising his index finger in the air to show me that he needs a minute.

"Do you want to know the truth?"

"Of course," I say slowly.

"You want to know the real reason why Nicholas will finally get what's coming to him?"

Shivers run down my spine. My hands turn to ice. I wait for him to continue.

"I turned him in," Owen says, laughing. "I did it. That's why they're after him."

I shake my head a little from side to

side, not wanting to believe the words that are coming out of his mouth.

"How…why?" I gasp.

"I called the main office and I told them what he did for Art Hedison."

"You mean what we did," I correct him.

"Yeah, except that I lied about that. I kept our names out of it. I had just enough information to get Internal Affairs involved and they opened a case on Art. To protect his own ass, Art turned on him, of course."

"So…that whole manhunt that they have on him, that's because of *you*?"

He nods and laughs.

"But why? He helped you so much."

"He was informing on me, Olive. To the fucking FBI! Or did you forget that?"

"Of course not, but we did that job together. He helped you a lot. He set us up with all of that money."

"Oh, please," Owen says, waving his hand. "I don't care about that. That guy killed my girlfriend and he almost stole you from me. I'm glad that I did what I did."

I walk over to him.

My mind goes blank.

My mouth goes dry.

My hand forms into a fist and I punch him straight in his nose.

When he yells out and wraps his hands around his head, I punch again.

As hard as I can.

My hand starts to throb, sending little shockwaves of pain up my arm but that just makes me even more angry.

He betrayed me just like Nicholas betrayed me but he did it out of spite.

His betrayal was worse.

"Get out of my fucking life!" I say on my way out.

19

OLIVE

On the way home, my hand feels incredibly hot. My fingers become sausages and it feels like they're about to blow up.

I turn up the air conditioner and hold them up in the vents.

At the stop light, I take a closer look and realize that they're not actually as big as they feel. But they definitely need some ice.

A few minutes later, I pull up to my driveway, but something stops me from actually going inside the garage.

The door opens and I wait.

Then I press the button on the sun shield and pull back out.

No, tonight I'm going out.

I need a drink and I'm not going to drink alone.

What I need even more than a drink is someone to talk to and a little bit of a distraction.

I don't know of any bars around here but I really liked the restaurant where I met with Josephine so I drive there.

There's a large parking lot in the back with not too many available spaces.

It's early fall and the snowbirds are just starting to come back to the desert.

I grab a seat on the edge of the bar so that I can see the beautiful vertical garden right across from me and ask the bartender for some ice in a bag.

"Had a bit of an accident," I lie.

He gives me a nod that says that he doesn't quite believe me so I don't bother elaborating.

I order the same cucumber tequila cocktail that I had earlier and find myself mesmerized as he makes it for me.

The bartender is in his thirties with short dirty blonde hair and sideburns. He's got tattooed sleeves on both arms.

We talk casually as the bar fills up and then empties out again.

He's originally from Orange County and moved out here so that he could afford to buy a house.

The housing prices are high everywhere in California but they are a little more reasonable in the Coachella Valley.

"I've lived in LA for many years but what I like about this Palm Springs area is that it's like all of the best parts of LA without any of the annoying things. Great restaurants and bars. Cool, easy going people. Cheaper rent and no traffic."

"Yeah, I heard traffic in LA can be brutal," I say, finishing my drink and asking for another.

"You're lucky you've been spared so far," he says, cutting up my cucumber and placing it carefully into a new glass.

While he serves the other customers

their drinks, I glance over at him occasionally.

I like the way he interacts with them. He's friendly and confident.

I like the way his hair falls into his face just a little bit.

I like the way he's at ease in making small talk and how natural it is for him.

There are very few things about him that should remind me of Nicholas.

He doesn't have the same intensity or darkness.

Yet, when I look at him, all I see is Nicholas.

It's getting late. The patrons are starting to file out and it's time for me to go as well.

But I can't make myself move.

I take the last few sips of my drink, which is all melted ice by now, and stare at the bottom of the glass.

"I think I'm ready to go," I say with great sadness.

I wait for him to tally my bill.

"Hey, I'm not closing out the bar tonight," he says.

I stare at him as if that's supposed to mean something.

"I get off in a few minutes," he explains. "You want to do something?"

I raise my eyebrows in surprise.

I had no idea he was particularly interested since he seemed to give all of his customers the same attention.

I glance down at my phone. It's around midnight.

This is probably the latest that I've been out in a very long time.

"I don't know," I mumble. "It's getting late."

"Sure." He shrugs.

He doesn't push.

He just gives me the bill to sign and walks away.

A pang of regret rushes through me.

Why did I say that? I like him. A lot. I'd love to spend some more time with him.

"What did you have in mind?" I ask, leaning over the bar.

His eyes light up.

"There's a coffee shop down the street that's open late."

That sounds perfect.

I go to the bathroom and reapply some lipstick.

A few minutes later, he meets me by the front door.

The night is warm but not balmy. I haven't been out much at night here but I enjoy the way the edge seems to be off from the burning sun of the day.

On our way to the coffee shop, he takes my hand in his. I'm taken aback at first, but then I let our fingers intertwine.

We slow down our pace and then something catches my eye in the store front of an antique shop.

It's a statue of a sheep made from bronze and covered in sheep fur.

The only bronze that's visible is on the face and the feet and I stand here staring at it for a long time.

"That's really cool," he whispers into my ear, breaking the spell.

I look up at him and nod.

Tilting his head forward, he puts his mouth on mine and I pull him closer.

We stand here kissing for a long time.

We pass on the coffee shop and instead go to his place. I follow him in my car. On the way over, I try to talk myself out of it but it doesn't work.

I want him. He wants me.

I can't have Nicholas.

We're kissing again before we clear the doorstep. His hands are down my back and mine are in his hair.

His lips are soft yet strong.

I realize that he doesn't know my name and I don't know his.

I consider pulling away and asking but we're already in the bedroom and I don't care.

With the lights out, surrounded completely by darkness, it's easier to pretend that he's Nicholas.

His kisses become urgent.

Our clothes seem to take off themselves.

When we're naked, his body warms me up and mine cools him down.

He kisses me everywhere and I do the same.

He isn't in a rush to get it done, and I appreciate it.

I haven't been touched like this in a very long time and I want it to last as long as possible.

We change positions once and then again and again.

I feel like we're dancing.

Our mouths are comfortable with each other now.

I start to unwind. I was relaxed before but not like this.

"Are you okay?" he whispers into my ear. I nod.

"More than okay. Keep doing that."

He does. Our bodies move as one and suddenly I lose all control.

20

NICHOLAS

WHEN I HAVE TO MAKE DECISIONS...

I wake up a few unrestful hours later with Mallory still in my bed.

She is curled up in the fetal position with her hair spread out all around her pillow.

She's beautiful and sweet and I don't want to get to know her more. It's not just because I'm running for my life. It's because she's not Olive.

I log into my account again, hoping against hope that what I saw before was some sort of mistake. Or maybe it was just a dream.

However, my hopes are low.

I didn't have enough money to pay for

my dinner so how the hell am I going to have enough money to pay for a ticket abroad?

Thailand.

That was the original plan.

There are lots of expats there but not so many American television programs to keep them entertained.

The country is huge and populous and it's easy to get lost there.

The feds have frozen my fake identity's account.

Art Hedison didn't know any of the details but he knew I had a source to make me the documents. Somehow, they must have gotten to him. That means that all of those identities he made for me are compromised.

Shit, shit, shit, I say to myself. I'm in a lot more trouble than I had thought.

Mallory gives out a little snore and turns around. I freeze for a moment, not wanting to wake her up while I try to figure out what to do.

That money was everything I had.

I sold the diamonds and the watch and

I put all of the money into what I thought was a secret and secure account.

I put the rest of my money in there, too. I didn't want to walk around with so much cash and the account was supposed to be completely safe.

I already spent whatever cash I took out from it and now I can't take out anymore.

If the account were to be unfrozen again, the money is still untouchable.

The Feds know about it and that means they will be able to track it.

I sit back in the chair and wonder if actually this was a lucky break. If they hadn't frozen it, then I'd still have access to it and I would use it.

If they hadn't frozen it, then they would be able to trace it to me.

It may be a lucky break but what the hell do I do now?

With all of my accounts compromised, I don't have a penny to my name. I won't be able to get far without money and I'm not sure how much I can borrow from Mallory.

We just met and she already did me more favors than she really should have.

I want to pace around the room to clear my head but I don't want to wake her up.

Instead, I sneak out of the front door with the room key and my phone in tow. It's early but the streets of Merida are already buzzing around. People are hustling to work. The coffee shops are full of locals and expats speaking ten different languages. Dogs and their owners are out on their morning constitutionals.

There's a large open square with a green park in the middle and a towering Catholic church painted in bright pastels to one side.

I take a few loops around the park, watching the way that the pigeons congregate and move as both individuals and one big mass. I don't have any seeds to throw them but I wish I did.

I take a seat on a wooden park bench and lean back. It's not particularly comfortable, which is probably for the best. I bought a cup of Cuban coffee from the shop on the corner and I take a sip. It's strong and sweet, kind of like a shot of espresso and a donut mixed in one.

I reach into my pocket for my phone and realize that I actually have two in there. In my rush to get out, I grabbed Mallory's by accident. I stare at my phone for a few minutes debating whether I should make this call with it.

My brain rationalizes, of course, they don't have this untraceable number, how could they?

But my gut is keeping it in check.

I don't have any proof that they are tracing my number but I also had no proof that they had access to my secret bank account. The only way to stay safe is to ditch this phone and use another.

I pick up Mallory's phone with a bright yellow cover and dial one of the numbers I know by heart.

Memorizing phone numbers is a dying art but I still practice it just in case.

A familiar voice answers.

He recognizes me immediately and we make small talk for a bit. Big Dipper sounds like he hasn't been to bed yet which wouldn't be at all surprising. He lives in Vegas and lives the Vegas lifestyle to the max.

"Listen, the reason I'm calling is that I need a job," I cut the chitchat short.

"What kind of job?"

"Anything. I need money."

"You're all over the news, man," Big Dipper says. "Everybody's looking for you. You're hot property."

"That's why I'm calling you. You owe me."

There's silence on the other end. I hold my breath waiting for his reply.

There was a time when the cops were after him, questioned me, and I set them off on a cold trail.

"I don't have any work right now," Big Dipper says after a moment. The tone of his voice makes me uneasy.

What if his phone is tapped, too?

"Are you sure?" I beg.

He's my only chance. If he doesn't help me, I'm out of options.

"Call me back in a bit. I'll ask around," he says and hangs up.

Not entirely sure what a little bit means, but I have to give it at least a few hours. I head back upstairs.

When I open the door, Mallory jumps out of bed.

"Are you okay?" I ask. She scrambles for the TV remote and before she can turn it off, I see my face on it.

Fuck!

"Hey, listen, I have to get back to work," she mumbles. "I mean, I have to get back home."

"Yeah, sure," I say, pretending that I didn't just see what I saw.

If she's trying to act inconspicuous, it's not working. But I'm not going to do anything to stop her. I don't want a confrontation and I'm definitely not going to hurt her (even though she seems to think that I will).

"Thanks for last night," I say.

"Oh, yes, of course," she says frantically. "It was nothing."

I wait for her to get fully dressed before I ask her.

"Do you think I can borrow some money?"

"Money?" All blood drains from her face.

I want to tell her to stop worrying and that I'm not going to hurt her, but that will just make things worse.

She looks through her purse and pulls out a few twenties. Dollars not pesos.

"Here, you can have this." She puts them in my hand a little too forcefully and heads toward the door.

"I'll get this back to you!" I yell after her.

"No need," she says quickly.

Once the door closes behind her, I can't help but feel like I had put her under a bit of duress.

I count the money: eighty dollars. A wave of relief sweeps over me. I've had millions but I've never felt this rich.

It takes me a few minutes to pack up and leave.

I don't know how long it will take

Mallory to call the hotline, or if she will at all, but I'm not planning on making it extra easy for them to find me by sticking around this place.

I wander the streets of Merida for a few hours, waiting for Big Dipper to call me back.

I have some vegetarian tacos and a few scoops of ice cream at a small cafe run by a Greek immigrant. I try to figure out what to do if Big Dipper doesn't come through.

One option is to rob someone to get more money, but then what?

I don't have any contacts here south of the border and there's a bounty out on my head that's worth hundreds of thousands.

I doubt that I'll be able to find one person who won't turn me over in exchange for all of that cash.

I call him after three that afternoon, again using Mallory's phone, which I forgot to give back to her.

"I got something," Big Dipper says. "But you're not going to like it."

21

NICHOLAS

WHEN I HAVE AN OPTION...

I already know that.

Of course, it's not going to be something fun or glamorous or safe. That's not the kind of jobs that Big Dipper is known for.

Yet, the fact that he is introducing it with that kind of preface makes my hands ball up into fists.

My heart jumps into my throat and I wait for him to explain

"I need a clean cut guy to drive some meth across the border from Mexico. A gringo with a white wife that the border agents won't stop because they have nothing to hide."

Fuck.

"You there?" Big Dipper asks.

"Yeah," I say after a moment.

"It's not the best option for you as you already know but that's all I got. Take it or leave it."

"Where would this be? Who am I going with?" I ask.

About a hundred more questions pop into my head but I keep it to two.

"I can't give any details until you commit to it. Why don't you think about it for a bit and let me know?"

I want to. I want to buy some time and try to figure something else out but I need papers. I need identification. My old source is compromised so Big Dipper is it.

"How much?" I ask.

There's a pause on the other end.

"How much meth or how much money?"

"Both."

"One hundred pounds of meth. I can pay you one fifty for it."

I do quick math in my head.

"The street value of that is about one

point three million. Getting it across the border for one fifty is a bargain."

"To some, it's enough to start a new life."

"I need at least two fifty," I negotiate. "And a whole new identity. Clean. Established. No dead people."

One way to get new social security numbers is to go through the list of the dead and just use their names hoping that the credit card companies won't notice.

It works in the short-term but that's not the kind I need.

I need a spanking new social security number that has been around at least thirty years and has no records or issues with it.

Then I need a whole new identity to go with it.

I need the Louis Vuitton or the Bentley of the identity business. And just like high end bags and cars, this one comes at a steep price.

"The best I can do is one seventy five and the ID. Take it or leave it."

I tap my foot on the floor.

The Mexican border is one of the most patrolled and highly secure places in the US. And trying to sneak over it with one hundred pounds of meth is about as stupid as anything I can think of. The only problem is that I don't have another choice.

I HEAD STRAIGHT TO A HAIR SALON ACROSS town. I found it on Yelp with good reviews. The owners are Japanese and they hire mainly Europeans to work there to cater to the expats in the area.

In broken Spanish, I ask for a whole new look and show the hairdresser pictures of celebrities with the kind of style I want.

He asks me a few times if I'm sure that this is what I want before getting started.

My hair is short but not army short.

It's thick and dark and I'm going with a look that's the exact opposite, dirty blond and long to match the sun-kissed tan that my skin recently acquired.

The color job along with the

extensions takes a few hours. In America, I wouldn't be able to afford it but here I will still have a lot of my money left even with a tip. In the meantime, I search on my phone for a place I can get colored contacts in the city.

I thought I would need to go to an optician but they sell them right in the open in beauty supply stores.

I haven't shaved in a few days and I plan to keep that look going. When I look at myself in a drugstore mirror, I look like a completely different person.

Older somehow and a bit of a slob, which is kind of in line with the part that I'll be playing: an expat living in Mexico.

Still, something feels off.

The hair that's coming in around my neck and face makes me look disheveled and a bit like a druggie, which is the last thing I want.

I head to a barber shop and show them pictures of freshly trimmed facial hair with an attractive mustache and a well-cared for beard.

They explain the details of the look to

me in Spanish, most of which I don't
understand.

At the end, they lay me back in the
chair and give me a shave. When they
hand me a mirror, I see a completely
different person, upscale, put together and
relaxed, the perfect look for my gringo
persona.

All I need to complete the look is a few
Hawaiian shirts and cargo shorts. I send
Big Dipper a selfie of my new face so that
he can get his guy to make me a passport.

I'm glad that it's going to be a day or
so before I cross the border as it will give
me some time to fill out my beard.

Big Dipper sends me a hysterical
laughing emoji with a thumbs up sign in
response.

A few hours later, he calls and tells me
that there has been a change of plans.

Now, instead of crossing into Texas, I
have to cross through California.

Tijuana is probably one of the most
heavily controlled border points along the
entire border.

"That's not a good idea," I say.

"The other shipment fell through," he says without offering much of an explanation.

"What do you mean?" I ask, even though it's in my best interest to know as little about his dealings as possible.

"Confiscated."

My heart skips a beat.

"You want to do this or not?"

"When do I meet the woman?"

"In Tijuana. She'll have your passport for you."

Tijuana? I look it up on my phone. It says it's 4100 km away. How far is that?

"Twenty-five hundred miles?" I ask. "How am I supposed to get there? I don't have a car and the roads around here are shit."

"That's up to you. But you better be there in seventy-two hours or else. Oh, yeah, and get a new fucking phone. Call me when you're there and I'll tell you about the meet-up place."

Big Dipper hangs up and I stare at the screen dumbfounded.

I don't have anywhere near the

amount of money I would need to buy a car and I doubt that I can hitch all the way there in time. I don't have any identification so I can't take a flight.

What a fucking shit show!

I guess the bus is the only way, I say to myself, gritting my teeth.

I've already taken one bus from Belize and even though some of them can be quite comfortable, it's not the best way to spend two days.

But given the time crunch, I'll have to get on the next one available, otherwise there's no fucking way I'll make it.

I look up the bus schedules online but don't buy my ticket electronically.

Mexico is still a heavy cash country and that's good for me.

I get rid of Mallory's phone but take out the SIM card and put it in one trash can and the rest of the phone in another, more than a mile away.

I do the same thing with mine.

I exchange my dollars for pesos and hope to God that it's enough for a one-way ticket to Tijuana.

There is no direct route and I'll have to change buses in Mexico City.

Honestly, I'm kind of surprised that I don't have to change more than that.

At the station, I buy a cheap disposable and untraceable phone and board the bus.

22

NICHOLAS

WHEN I COMMUTE...

The bus is much more pleasant than I expect. It has air conditioning, comfortable seats, and a television.

It's in Spanish but they keep showing American movies from a few years ago so I've either seen them or can follow the basic plot.

I grab the seat in the middle and keep to myself.

Luckily, the other people do, too.

The only time I ever even make eye contact with someone is when we're both waiting to use the restroom at the same time.

The bus makes occasional stops at

various stations and I follow the rest of the passengers out to get homemade tamales and other things that the local venders stands are selling.

When I need a pick-me-up, I opt for the fresh-squeezed juice, mango and mandarin are my favorites.

The journey is long and boring and at one station I spot a few paperbacks in English.

They are dirt cheap so I splurge on four. They are mostly by authors I've never heard of, but I don't care. Without a smartphone, I don't have access to my audiobooks, podcasts, movies, books, or music.

It has been thirty hours of nothing but listening to the thoughts in my own head. That's enough for me.

Most of my thoughts are just those of regret and what-ifs.

The majority come back to Olive.

I need something to entertain me.

Finally, we arrive in Tijuana. A dusty border town that's known for its hookers and drugs. I'm surprised to see that there's a whole other part of Tijuana as well. There are expensive coffee shops, restaurants and boutiques, and high rise condos gentrifying neighborhoods.

The bus station is a new beautiful building with glass walls and murals on one side.

It's a bustling place full of vendors and all sorts of people coming and going.

Expecting a dusty outpost at the edge of the world, I am pleasantly surprised.

I call Big Dipper as soon as I step off the bus and find a quiet corner. He is happy to hear from me.

"Another few hours and you would've lost the job," he warns.

"Why is there such a time crunch?"

"I'm a subcontractor. There are a lot of people vying for this job. If I can't deliver, they move on to another group. There is no holding it. Not for you, not for anyone."

He didn't have to say this to remind me that we are not friends. We've met a few times in Vegas, had a few good times, but we are nothing but business associates.

"Don't forget that I saved your life once." I remind him of the debt that he owes me.

In this line of work, your word is your bond.

"That's why I offered you the opportunity in the first place," he says. "You'll meet Dorothy at the Starbucks upstairs in half an hour. She'll have the rest of the details."

"What does she look like?" I ask, but Big Dipper already hung up.

I FIND THE STARBUCKS, GET A CUP OF coffee, and take a seat by the window. I scan each face that comes in and out and search them to see if they are looking for me.

As you would expect, most women getting coffee in a bus station are frazzled and in a hurry.

No one is just hanging around and waiting.

I leave my spot for a few minutes to use

the restroom and when I come back, I
see her.

Is that her? No, that can't be her. She's
in her forties, or maybe fifties even.

"Are you Liam?" she asks.

For a second, I forget the name that
Big Dipper has assigned me.

"Yes, I am. Dorothy?"

"Oh, yes, what a relief!" she says,
collapsing into the chair across from me.

"Can I get you something to drink?" I
offer.

"Yes, of course. I'll have a latte." I
don't have much money left, and the few
dollars deplete my savings considerably but
I don't want to be an asshole. Not off
the bat.

I need to talk to her. I don't want to
make pleasantries but I need to speak to
her about what we're about to do.

When her drink is ready, I ask her to
take a walk with me.

On the off chance that someone is
following us, we will just look like two
people taking a stroll around the bus
station.

If they were to try to listen in on our conversation, that would be even more difficult. Unless…

Of course, I need to protect myself. I lead her out of the bus station and duck into a nearby alleyway.

"I think it would be best if we show each other that we are not wired," I say. "Before we talk."

She thinks about it for a moment and then gives me a nod.

She pulls up her shirt, exposing her black bra, and I let out a sigh of relief. I show her my torso and she gives me a nod.

We exchange phones and check them for recordings as well, also finding nothing.

"Okay, let's walk," I say.

We decide to call each other by our given name in order to shroud ourselves in an additional level of protection. Without a name, there's no one to turn on.

"So, what's their plan?" I ask.

"You don't know?"

I shrug. "Big Dipper said you would tell me."

"Basically, tonight, during rush hour

when all of the other expats are coming back into the US, we'll get into the RV that they got for us and get over the border."

"That's it?" I ask.

"That's all I know. They said the details are up to us. We can be a married couple or girlfriend and boyfriend or whatever, just as long as we cross the border successfully that's all they care about."

"Of course, that's all they care about. They aren't going to be the ones facing years in prison if they get caught."

"Years?" Her mouth drops open.

"Yes, of course! That's one hundred pounds of methamphetamine. That's going to be one hell of a loot if they catch us with it."

Dorothy hangs her head and slouches her shoulders, suddenly aging thirty years.

"I don't know if I can do this," she whispers.

23

NICHOLAS

WHEN I TRY TO CONVINCE HER...

My heart starts to pound but I don't let it show. I need her to do it and, if I want to convince her, I can't look desperate.

"It's going to be okay, Dorothy. We'll have a great cover story—"

"Which is?" she asks, folding her arms across her chest.

"We're dating. We've been dating for a while. You want me to propose but I don't want to be tied down. I'm not a cheater but I'm just one of those guys who doesn't need a piece of paper to define who he loves."

She leans against the wall and props up

her foot as well. Dressed in flip-flops and a long flowing dress, she looks exactly like someone who would vacation down in Baja.

"Why are we coming back?" she asks.

"Your mother fell down again," I say without missing a beat. "We're coming to check on her."

"Where do we live most of the time?"

"The RV. We're full-timers. At least, for the last year and a half. We love life on the road. We love meeting new people and seeing new places."

I tell her all of this and a lot more. The story comes out of my mouth so easily I feel like I've told it a million times before.

"How do you feel now?"

"I still don't feel too good about having so much …of that stuff in there," she says in a quiet whisper.

I shrug. "Me either, but no one else is going to pay us that much money to drive an RV across the border."

My confidence and my story seems to put her at ease and she shows me the address that she got from Big Dipper.

When we look it up, it's just a few streets over. The RV is not particularly big but, luckily, it looks like it has been through a lot.

With our story, we need our home to look like it has more than a few miles on it. The inside is filled up with clothes and junk, just enough so that it looks like it's well lived in.

"This thing is perfect," I say, sitting behind the wheel. The door is unlocked and there are two men in a car a block away watching us. They must've been the ones who dropped it off.

"Where is it?" Dorothy asks.

I shrug.

"I thought you would know."

"I don't." She shakes her head.

A part of me is tempted to look for it, but another part just wants to drive and get this over with.

"They wouldn't have left it somewhere that is easy to find, would they?" Dorothy asks.

"Not if they don't want it confiscated.

The dogs will also be making their way around."

Dorothy's eyes get big and I realize that I've said enough.

"Typically with marijuana they hide it with coffee. I'm not sure what they do with meth but they want it to arrive there safely. They aren't setting us up."

My voice is confident, but on the inside I'm full of doubt.

There is a warrant out for my arrest.

What if this is just a big ruse?

No, Big Dipper wouldn't do that.

Why would he want to lose one hundred pounds of meth in the process when he could just call the Feds and report on me directly?

Or what if that's a lie, too?

It's rush hour and, according to Google Maps, it's going to take at least two hours to cross the border at this pace.

Everyone is crawling.

The sun is beating down on us and the air conditioning in this thing leaves much to be desired.

Suddenly, I'm not at all charmed by all of this rig's imperfections.

"I had better AC on the bus on the way here," I say.

Dorothy looks out in the distance, barely registering what I'm saying.

I try the radio but none of the upbeat Mexican music appeals to me so I turn it off.

"So, how did you get into this line of work?" I ask after we come to a complete stop once again.

She slowly turns to me, brushing her hair out of her face.

Our eyes meet briefly but then she looks away.

I want to ask her if she's okay but I don't want to give her the opportunity to tell me that she doesn't want to do this again.

"My husband," she finally says. "He's really sick. Cancer."

"I'm so sorry."

"Stage three. Liver. There are some options for treatment but they aren't great. And they're really expensive."

Traffic speeds up a bit and we enjoy a steady pace of about ten miles an hour but only for a few minutes.

"There are some experimental treatments available at private clinics. There are no guarantees but I want him to fight. He has been fighting but things don't look good."

"So, why are you doing this?" I ask.

"Money, why does anyone do anything? These treatments are promising but they cost money. Insurance won't cover them. We already got a second mortgage to cover the chemotherapy but it's nowhere near enough to try this. And I'm not going to lose him over something as stupid as money."

I nod. Why does it always come to that? Why does everything seem to revolve around a few pieces of paper that someone infused with value?

I hear the anger in her voice and I feel her pain.

I don't understand it because I'm not going through it but I sympathize and I wish there was something I could do to make things right.

"That's why this has to work," she says, her fingers trembling. "We have to make it work."

We drive in silence all the way to the booth. My heart is pounding out of my chest when we get there. An alert agent dressed with a stern look on his face comes up to my driver's side.

"Passports please," he says.

24

NICHOLAS
WHEN WE CROSS THE BORDER...

I hand the officer my passport and then turn to Dorothy and say, "C'mon, hurry up. It's not like you didn't have three fucking hours to get it out."

She cringes and searches for hers in the glove compartment.

"What was your business in Mexico?" he asks.

"We're full-time RVers," Dorothy pipes in. "We sold our house last year and got this rig here, and we love it."

"She got a name?" he asks, looking at my passport. For a second, I hesitate. She? What is he talking about?

"Of course, she does!" Dorothy says,

handing him her passport. "Sorry about that, we had an issue and we had to get the manual out. Well, you know what that's like, right? Everything in that thing gets all jumbled up."

"Uh-huh," he says, looking at her passport.

"Freedom!" Dorothy yells over me.

"Ma'am?" he asks.

"Freedom. That's the name of our RV. Isn't it beautiful?"

"Yes, it is," he says rather disinterested.

"Okay, well, everything seems to be in order here. Wait for a moment while we get the dog to sniff around."

He walks away before either of us can say a word.

We exchange knowing looks and hold our breath.

When the dog finishes with the car up front, his handler brings him over to us.

I relax my hands around the steering wheel and fiddle around with the radio.

Dorothy suddenly seems to clam up. To snap her out of it, I pick an argument.

We've been together for years so it should be no big deal for us to argue in public.

"When I get back, I'm going to go to the gym first," I announce. "I'll drop you off at your mother's and meet up with you later."

It takes her a second to respond but then she does.

"You're not going to see my mother?" she gasps. "We've driven all this way and you're not even going to stop in?"

"I will, in an hour or so. I need to unwind. Besides, *we* didn't drive all this way. *I* drove all this way," I correct her. "And you just don't want to go see her on your own. And you know that. I'm your buffer."

"You are not a buffer!" she yells.

"You're all set. Have a safe trip," the border agent says, tapping the side of the RV. I drive away and pull my window up, but we don't stop arguing until we are a few miles away for safe measure.

"D<small>ID THAT JUST HAPPEN</small>?" I <small>TURN TO</small>
Dorothy with a wide smile on my face. She
nods, letting out a high-pitched squeal and
claps her hands. She pulls out a Twix from
her purse and offers to split it with me.

"No, thanks," I say.

"It's our celebratory candy bar!"
Dorothy says. "Milk chocolate. Caramel.
It's delicious. C'mon, you know you
want it."

"It's all yours," I say, shaking my head.

She bites into it feverishly, picking off
the little crumbs that fall on her shirt.

"Where are we going now?" I ask
when her phone beeps. The drop-off
location is about twenty miles north.

"What are you going to do now?" I ask
after a long period of silence. "Go home to
San Diego?"

"How long will the money last with the
cancer treatments?" I ask.

She bites her lower lip. "A little bit but
not long."

"What are you going to do then?"

"Probably this, again," she says,

looking out in the distance. "What else is there?"

We look at the desert stretching wide before us. The sky is bright blue and the land is a dusty beige, and it's the most beautiful place in the world.

"Will you go with me?" she asks. We've been lucky once.

"I can't. This is it for me."

"Too bad."

"Dorothy, you've got to be smart about this. If you do this again, and that should be a big if, you need to go to Arizona or Texas or somewhere far away from this border."

"Why?"

"You can't risk getting the same agent. He won't believe your story the second time, if you're coming in with a different *boyfriend*."

"I'll think about it," she says under her breath.

I want to shake her. I want to tell her not to press her luck.

What happened back there was short

of a miracle and miracles don't tend to happen in sequence.

We arrive at the drop spot a few minutes later. It's the parking lot of a Walmart. Big, spacious, and not very full. I park in the back. We are to leave the keys in the RV, go inside, shop, and then come out.

I'm nervous about leaving it unlocked but spot two guys sitting in their old beat-up truck, watching me. They are waiting for it.

"How are we going to get the money?" Dorothy keeps asking me as we walk around the aisle aimlessly.

"They're going to drop it off," I say.

"What if they don't?"

I would be lying if that thought hadn't crossed my mind.

But there isn't much I can do. I don't really want to hold on to all of that meth for any longer than necessary.

"We should just be patient," I say.

Her eyes meet mine in the grocery section. She's worried, much more than I am.

My goal was to get into the US. If it all goes to shit, I can go to Vegas and find Big Dipper and try to set things right.

But Dorothy? She doesn't really know him as anyone but a voice on the phone.

And she needs the money to save her husband's life.

25

NICHOLAS

WHEN WE WAIT...

We come out of the store, holding our shopping bags full of snacks, food, and water. Most of them are mine.

I lead Dorothy to the bus stop all the way across the parking lot. This would be the least conspicuous place to do this.

"The RV is gone," Dorothy says, turning to me.

"They are going through it."

"They took it and they aren't going to pay us," she says, shaking her head.

It's a very real possibility, I admit, but keep my mouth shut. I don't want to make her worry anymore than she already is.

We wait for close to ten minutes, which feels like a decade.

Then the same car, but this time with just one guy pulls up to us. He doesn't get out.

He just stops, opens the door, and gives us each a duffel bag, then drives away.

I open the zipper and peer inside. Seeing bundles of cash makes my heart sing. This is going to be enough to get a new identity, a clean one, and to start a new life.

"It's all here," Dorothy says, overjoyed, after doing a rudimentary count of the money. "What are you going to do now?"

"Get a cab and a ride to a used car dealership. You can't get around California well without one. You?"

"Same thing, I guess. Minus the car dealership."

"You're going to take the cab all the way to San Diego?" I ask. She shrugs. "With all of that money?"

She shrugs again.

"No, come with me and I'll give you a ride."

I BUY A 2006 HONDA ACCORD FOR AN even three grand, splurging a bit on one that has a sound transmission so that it doesn't break down at some inconvenient time on the freeway.

After dropping off Dorothy at her house, I call Big Dipper.

"When are all of my papers going to be ready?" I ask as soon as he answers.

"Good job. It's nice to hear from you, too," he says.

"Sorry about that, it has been a long day."

"I need a few more days," Big Dipper says.

"A few more days? I thought I could fly out tomorrow."

"No can do. The guy's wife is having a baby."

"What?" I ask, half laughing. I was expecting any sort of excuse but not that one.

"Yep, it's the world we live in. She's

having a baby and he's there for her, doesn't matter what shit is going down."

I chuckle, shaking my head.

"Besides, maybe it's a good thing. Airport security is tight. You're going to have to be invisible if you want to get out by air."

"Even with the new ID?" I ask.

"Go online and Google yourself, you'll see. You better just go somewhere quiet and lay low. And by low, I mean real low. No friends. No acquaintances. No girls. Oh, man, your life is going to suuuuuuuck!"

After I hang up, I drive to a cell phone store and buy myself a proper smartphone.

I pay cash and register it using the passport that I used to cross the border.

Back in the parking lot, I look myself up online.

Big Dipper wasn't lying.

The number of programs and articles that feature my name have more than doubled since I was in Belize.

It would be a death wish to try to fly

out of LAX or any other airport with all of their facial recognition software.

The only reason I even got back into the US is that no government agency thought I'd be so stupid as to come back here.

"Fuck me," I say. "What the fuck am I going to do now?"

I start the engine and drive. Turning onto the Pacific Coast Highway, I drive along with the wide ocean to one side. The moon is huge and bright yellow today, casting shadows over the quiet waves out by the horizon.

It has been a very long day and I should probably get a hotel room somewhere but I can't stop driving.

I put on some classic rock and lose myself in Bob Dylan and the Rolling Stones.

My grip on the steering wheel is relaxed and I sit back comfortably in the weathered leather seat.

There are about a hundred and twenty-thousand miles on this car. I wonder where has it been in its whole life? Did it travel across the country and if so, how many times? Or did it only drive over the same twenty miles from home to work over and over again?

In my heart, I hope it has seen some adventure. Cars, after all, are meant to go places.

Speaking of going places, where should I go now? Two directions are out of the question. I'm not going back south and I can't physically go west unless I take a plane. So, it's either north or east for me.

It doesn't take long for my thoughts to drift back to Olive.

Whenever I relax or don't have anything pressing to think about, they always come back to her.

When I see a sign to go east, I take that road and it takes me away from the ocean. I know where she is and now that there are less than two hours separating us, I feel her gravitational pull.

I can't get there fast enough.

I don't want to speed but at seventy

miles an hour, I feel like I'm driving through molasses.

Finally, an hour later, I start seeing signs for desert cities. A little bit later, I pass Cabazon Outlets and I finally see the windmills that separate Palm Springs from the rest of Southern California.

The windmills are tall and numerous. At night, they are practically invisible except for the bright red blinking lights at the top. They are positioned in a valley between two desert mountain ranges, an optimal place for the great winds to gather and sweep through.

It's a particularly windy day and my car starts to shake from the pressure.

I grab on to the steering wheel a little harder to keep it in its place.

I've been to LA a number of times but I have never been to Palm Springs. How can anyone live here with all of this wind? I wonder to myself.

But everything changes when I get onto Palm Canyon Drive. Here, the palm trees barely sway in the breeze and people are happily enjoying their food outside.

Behind the restaurants and the parking lots, there's a huge mountain towering over the canyon. The same mountain that funnels the wind up north is now the one that's blocking all of it.

I put in the address that I remember belonged to Olive's mother.

It's the only address I have.

I can't very well reach out to my own investigator.

He's a little bit too good at finding people and that's the last person I want on my trail right now.

I pull up a long driveway and drive past her gate without stopping. At the top of the hill, there's a little turn out.

I park right up front, a little bit on the road, if I were telling the truth. But from this vantage point I can see people coming in and out of her house.

Then I wait.

An hour later, I feel like a total fool.

What are the chances that she even looked her mother up yet? And even if she did, that doesn't mean that she would be at her house at this time. Still, I want to stay longer but my eyelids start to feel heavier.

The one thing I can't do is fall asleep here. Still, I wait.

A few hours later, I drive away.

26

OLIVE

WHEN I MEET THEM...

I change my outfit about five times before I settle on the right one. For some reason I am more nervous to meet *them* than I was to meet her.

Well, no, that's not true. I was dying inside the first time I went to see Josephine. Still, meeting her husband and kids is a big deal. I wasn't expecting us to get to that level so fast.

I finally show up at their house in a collared dress with a belt around the front. It's dressy but not very fancy. After going back and forth between flip-flops and heels, I finally settle on wedge sandals.

Josephine meets me at the door and

gives me a warm hug. Two little kids are playing in the living room. One is four and the other is two. I kneel down next to them.

Ellen, the older one, shows me her cars and Byron, the younger boy, shows me his sticker collection.

I love how informal their presence is making this whole interaction. We don't shake hands, we just dive right in. Josephine stands a little bit away from me, watching us lovingly.

"Where's your daddy?" I ask Byron. He just points to the kitchen and grunts. Ellen laughs, so does Josephine.

"He'll be out in a minute," Josephine says.

"Of course, no rush," I say, sitting back in the bean bag chair and admiring my siblings.

I don't know if Josephine would want me thinking of them as that yet but I already do and I'm falling in love with them.

"Olive! I'm so sorry, I was on a call." A

man about Josephine's age comes out to greet me.

He has kind eyes, a strong fit body, and a smile that lights up the whole room. He gives me a warm hug and a kiss on the cheek.

"Come on, let's sit. Can I get you a drink?" he asks.

"Wallace makes the best Old-fashioneds."

"I'll have to try that."

"Jo caught me up on everything that has happened but I'd love to hear more about you," Wallace says when we take our seats in the living room. "And by the way, I am so, so sorry that this happened. Ever since I've known Jo, she has been looking for you. And I'm sorry that you two didn't have each other all of these years."

His words bring tears to my eyes and I can't hold them back. They are so unexpected and loving that I'm physically overwhelmed.

I spend most of the dinner talking about myself after they ask question after question about my experiences growing up.

I'm torn between telling them the whole truth and covering up some of it with lies. I know that the whole truth will hurt Josephine even more than she already is and I want to protect her from some of the pain. But she always deserves to know what really happened to her daughter.

Luckily, over dessert, the kids start to dominate the conversation and I find myself slipping off the hook.

I play with them.

I talk to them.

I ask them about their lives and Ellen fills me on both of theirs.

"I think it's getting late," I say a few hours later.

I don't really want to go but I also don't want to overstay my welcome.

"We're actually going to put Byron to bed and have Ellen do some quiet time, but can you stay just for a little bit longer?" Josephine asks. "We can have some more drinks out on the patio."

"Sure," I say, walking over to the sliding glass door.

"We'll be right back. Feel free to go out there if you want," Wallace says.

After kissing the kids goodnight, I watch them all disappear down the long hallway and I feel like I'm totally alone.

The valley is lit up by a million small lights. The views go around the wrap-around porch and are absolutely breathtaking.

When I glance up, I see that the house is practically etched into the mountain behind it.

I follow the curve of the pool, around the built-in hot tub with a cascading waterfall in front of it, and toward the other side.

The lights out front don't reach this far, and it takes me a moment to adjust to the darkness in this corner of the backyard.

"Aren't you going to introduce me to them?" Owen asks. For a second, I think I'm hearing things.

But when my eyes adjust to the

darkness, I see him. He's standing in the doorway of their pool house.

"What are you doing here?" I run over to him and push him inside.

"Why are you *here?*"

I look back hoping that they will take a little bit longer inside.

"Just wanted to check up on my sister and see how she's doing."

"You made it perfectly clear that I'm not your sister anymore," I snap.

"Well, I thought that maybe we could go back to that."

I see that as my chance. "Yes, we can," I say. "I just want you to get out of here."

"No," he says loudly. "Come to think of it, I'd much rather have you as something more than a sister."

"Lower your voice," I whisper, trying to offset his booming sound with the quietness of my own.

It doesn't work.

"Why haven't you been returning my calls?" he asks.

"We had a fight, Owen. I don't want to talk to you."

"Whatever," he says, waving his hand and sitting on their bed.

"Get up!" I grab him to pull him up, but instead he just pulls me down on top of him.

"Get off me!" I yelp, but he puts his hand on my mouth.

I bite down as hard as I can. He screams out in pain and slaps me square across my face. My cheek burns like it has been lit on fire and something starts to ooze out of my nose.

When I taste the iron, I realize that I have a bloody nose.

Before I can stop him, I'm on the bed, flat on my back, and he's on top of me.

"Get off," I whimper but he doesn't budge.

Instead, he pins my hands back, towering over me.

"Tonight, you're mine," he whispers into my ear and pulls out a gun. "If you don't do as I say, I'm going to kill that new family of yours."

27

OLIVE

WHEN I STAY QUIET…

M y mind goes blank. My body stops moving and resisting.

I just got my mother back. I'm not going to do anything to hurt her. I'm not going to do anything that will hurt my brother and sister.

"That's more like it," he says, relaxing his grip a little around my hands but not on the gun. "Now, you're going to do exactly as I say or they die."

"What guarantee do I have that you're not going to kill them…after?" I ask, keenly aware of my parched mouth.

"You don't. But I'll let you go if I have a good time here."

Blood drains away from my face.

My fingers get ice cold and so do my feet. He feels my body as if I have given my consent.

Thoughts rush around in my head.

Mostly, they are memories of what he used to be like.

How can this really be the man I used to know?

How can this really be the man who I wrote all of those letters to in prison and who wrote me all of those letters back?

He used to be someone I admired and now he's someone I despise.

I smell liquor on his breath. He's drunk but he has a high tolerance.

Still, he knows exactly what he's doing. His hands move around my body as I try to figure out what to do.

I can't let this happen but I also can't let him hurt Josephine or her family.

I have a lot of regrets in my life and that won't be one of them.

He starts to kiss my lips, my mouth, and my face. When he starts to move down my neck, he whispers, "Kiss me back."

I don't want to, but I can't say no.

I have to buy more time.

I need to figure this out.

There must be a way out.

I want to bite him, but I force myself to kiss him back.

He doesn't seem to notice that I'm doing it under duress.

"Yes, isn't that amazing, Olive? Is that everything you have dreamed of?" he mumbles and kisses me again.

I press my lips to his, I slowly open my eyes and glance down.

I can't see for sure but it feels like he's no longer holding onto the gun. I move my body and he moves his on top of me.

He thinks that I'm under his spell when all I'm doing is trying to find an angle.

When he grabs at my chest, I jerk away and head butt him with my head. He winces from the pain but it's not enough to keep him away.

He pins me down again but I wrestle out of his grasp. I search around the bed for the gun but I can't find it.

I try to kick him but his body is draped too closely over mine.

Then he does it again.

He presses his forearm against my throat.

My airway tightens and I start gasping for breath. I start to see stars and then my vision gets blurry.

When everything goes black, he finally lets me go. My throat burns with each cough.

"Don't you ever do that again, Olive," he sneers.

I glare at him.

Air starts to come back, clearing my cloudy thoughts.

He's on top of me again, not choking me but trying to take off my clothes.

I feel around my side for anything sharp or hard I can use to protect myself. But my fingers find nothing but clumps of sheets.

And then…

It's so cool and hard, it's hard to believe it's there and it's hard to confuse it with anything else. I grab the gun and push the barrel into his body. When I pull the trigger, he lets out a yell, grabbing onto his stomach.

"Olive, give me the gun," someone says over and over again while I stand over Owen writhing around in pain.

He repeats himself a number of times before I register the fact that it's Wallace who is speaking.

"The police are on their way," Josephine whispers. "He won't hurt you again."

At some point, I give up the gun.

At some point, the paramedics throw one of those gray blankets over me to keep me warm.

At some point, they put Owen on a stretcher and start to roll him away.

At some point, Josephine takes me into her arms, kisses my head, and tells me that everything is going to be okay.

The police don't give me a lot of time to rest before they come at me with their questions.

Josephine and Wallace walked in on me standing with the gun pointed at Owen after I had already shot him. No one here knows who he is and, for a moment, I debate whether they should.

"Oh, no, what did he do to you?" Josephine asks, tugging at the blanket around my neck and looking at the bruises.

I drop it to the floor and show them everything.

There's no point in hiding it.

If I lie or try to protect him, they are going to arrest me.

They document my bruises. They take pictures and make notes.

There are a lot more than I even thought I had.

There are those around my neck where he tried to strangle me.

There are those on my arms where he pinned me down.

There are those on my legs when I fought back.

There is even a visible mark on my cheek from when he slapped me and my nose started to bleed.

I describe what happened in as much detail as I can.

There are some parts of the attack that I don't quite remember the order of but everything else is crystal clear.

"I wanted to freeze but then he would've gotten what he wanted," I say at the end. "And I couldn't let him do that to me."

The detectives are cold and unresponsive but at least Josephine and Wallace believe me.

"And how did he know you were here?" one of the police officers asks.

"He knew that I came to Palm Springs to find my mother. I had her address and he saw it."

"And he's your boyfriend?"

I shake my head. "He's my brother," I say quietly. There's an audible gasp at that revelation.

"But he knew for a long time that we weren't really related. Something I only found out recently."

There is so much more to say and so much more to keep to myself.

But it's not Owen I want to protect.

It's Nicholas.

Owen has made his bed. He tried to rape me, he promised to kill my real mother and her family.

But the more I tell them about why we're here, the more likely they are to find our connection to Nicholas.

"And what is your attacker's name?" one of them asks and then I freeze.

28

OLIVE

WHEN I MAKE A DECISION...

The police officer asks me for Owen's name again. And then again. And again.

At first, I thought it would be so easy to go ahead and just tell them the truth, but then doubts creep in. I want him so badly to be the person that I thought he was that I almost can't come to terms with who he really is.

"Ma'am, what is his name?" a detective asks.

I can tell that they are growing impatient. Josephine puts her arm around me and asks them to give us a second.

"What's wrong? Why won't you tell them?"

Tears start to stream down my face.

"I just never thought that he would ever do that to me. I thought that he was someone I could trust. I waited so long for him to get out of prison and then out of that coma…" My voice trails off as I gasp for air in the middle of my sobs.

But touching my neck, I flinch.

"He tried to strangle you, Olive," Josephine says in her soothing, kind voice.

I nod.

"He tried to rape you. He would have succeeded if you hadn't shot him. He deserves everything that's coming to him."

"I know that's true. Of course, I do."

"So, what's holding you back?"

I swallow hard. When I look up at her, I lose myself for a moment in the blue of her irises. There's a deepness there that makes my whole body shake.

"You can do it," she whispers into my ear.

I open my mouth to say it but another cop interrupts me.

"His name is Owen Kernes and he's her brother," he reports.

"Your brother tried to rape you?" the detective asks.

"Yes, but he's not my biological brother."

Didn't I say that already? I wonder.

Suddenly, I have an out of body experience. I find myself telling the story or part of the story of my life but it doesn't feel like it's me saying it. Instead, I'm just watching this lost little girl with a blanket around her shoulders tell a bunch of strangers in uniform things that she hasn't told anyone before.

As the detectives turn their attention to Wallace, I pull away from Josephine and walk toward the ambulance.

Someone stops me from climbing in but not before I yell, "Why did you do that? Why did you do any of that?"

Owen doesn't respond.

"Why?" I scream, pounding my fists on the back of the ambulance.

"'Cause nothing matters without you,

Olive," he says slowly. "Don't you get that?"

"No." I shake my head.

"I don't have a life without you," he says.

The paramedics close the door and someone moves me out of the way. Big tears rush down my face, and I sit down and bury my face in my hands.

AFTER A WHILE, THE POLICE OFFICERS leave. I'll probably have to answer more questions and provide more explanations but for now they leave me alone. Josephine offers me some tea and a Xanax but I just accept the tea.

"I am really sorry about all of this," I tell both of them in the kitchen. The kids are luckily asleep and have slept through all of it.

I am sure that they are tempted to ask me to rehash everything that has happened but luckily, they don't. I don't have the energy to go over it one more time.

"I think I better get home. I need some sleep."

"No, no, no," Josephine says. "Please, stay in our guest room. It's all set up already."

"Only if you want to," Wallace says, giving me an out.

"Okay, but only if it's not a big imposition," I agree.

The room is spacious, about the size of a master bedroom in a normal house. It has its own bathroom and a walk-in closet. Wallace shows me where they keep the towels and Josephine comes in with an armful of sweats.

"I'm sure you want to change your clothes. Let me know if they're not a good fit and I'll try to find something else."

"I'm sure they're fine," I assure them and we bid each other goodnight.

I take off the clothes that the police had given me after they photographed me and took mine for evidence. I step directly into the shower and melt onto the floor.

My tears mix with the rushing water, alleviating some of my pain. I feel so alone

and there's only one person who can make
it all go away and he's not here.

My thoughts return to Nicholas.

"Where are you?" I ask. "Why aren't
you here? Why did you listen when I told
you to go? Why didn't you stay and fight?"

IN THE MORNING, AT FIRST LIGHT, I GET UP
and sneak out of their house. I leave them
a note thanking them for everything they
have done and telling them that I need
some time alone. At the end, I promise to
stay in touch.

I don't tell them where I'm going
because I don't know myself.

All I know is that I need some space.

I need to go somewhere to clear my
head.

The cops told me to stay close in case
they have more questions but I'll just come
back if they do.

I'm not running away, I'm going
somewhere to find myself again.

29

OLIVE

WHEN I TRY TO CLEAR MY HEAD...

I drive for a very long time. I don't know where I'm going and I don't really want to. When early dawn turns to midday, I turn up the air conditioning and keep driving.

When I get hungry, I pull over to a truck stop and wander the aisle looking for something healthy to eat. Stale donuts and old candy should be appetizing but for some reason they're not.

I grab a water and get back in the car.

What am I looking for? I don't know.

My life lies ahead of me but I don't know where it's going to take me. I can do anything and yet I feel like doing nothing.

I continue up the Pacific Coast Highway, watching the waves crash against themselves down the hills below. Every few miles there's a turnaround and people pull over and take pictures.

A small collection of shops congregates around the bend. I don't know exactly where I am except that it's somewhere in central California. The shops are small, more like shacks and I stop into one to buy some fruit and a cup of juice.

I walk down to the sand and drink my juice with my feet buried deep under the cold coarse sand. The wind coming off the ocean sends shivers through me and I wish I had a warmer sweater, but it also wakes me up. I stare out at the horizon and lose myself in it for a long time.

When I drink the last drop, my body feels full and energized, but my mind is no less muddled. A part of me wants to go back home, not just because it's the only place that feels familiar, but yet another part wants to go to Hawaii on the off chance that he's there.

I've been trying to put Nicholas out of

my mind for a long time but it's just not working. I thought that him not being on social media would make things easier. But for some reason, it has made this whole process more insufferable.

He is gone.

Vanished.

And the more that the FBI, the police, and who knows who else is looking for him, the further away he seems to be.

If they can't find him, how can I?

I am sure that there are many women out there right now who would love nothing more than to be actually cut off from contact with their ex. No phone number to text after a few glasses of wine, no social media posts to drool over or get jealous of.

Well, at first I thought I was one of the lucky ones.

I can't contact him and that means that if I want him out of my life, he is out of my life.

But now?

Now that I really can't contact him, I'm suddenly full of regret.

I wish there was more that was said.

I wish that I wasn't so angry that night, that I'd actually listened to what he was trying to tell me. I wish that I had been strong enough to tell him that I love him and just let it be known.

Somewhere in the distance, I see a guy walk excitedly holding his surfboard. His suit starts at his ankles and zips up all the way to his neck, leaving only his feet, hands, and head free.

The ocean in California is cold year round. I thought that if it's seventy-five degrees outside, the water would be warm like it is in Florida. But the currents come from Alaska and the coastline is very deep so if you want to spend any considerable time in the water, you have to wear a wet suit.

The surfer pulls on the zipper up his back to close it shut before giving me a slight nod and running into the waves.

Suddenly, a wave of nostalgia sweeps over me.

I remember walking on that warm Hawaiian beach and seeing Nicholas for the first time, before I even knew he was Nicholas.

It seems like that happened a million years ago and maybe to someone else altogether.

Is that possible?

I bury my hand in the cool sand and stumble upon a shell which is smooth like glass on the inside. Spinning it around in my fingers, I think about Nicholas.

I miss him much more than I want to admit.

I miss his lips. I miss his touch.

But the thing that I miss most is his presence.

There's a calmness to him. Whatever I might be going through, I'd feel like it was going to be okay just because he was there.

All I want to do now is just tell him about everything that has happened. He was the one who was supposed to be here when I met my real mother. He was the one that found her.

My phone vibrates in my pocket.

It's Josephine.

I'm tempted to not answer. I reach to press the 'ignore' button.

"Hi, sorry I left so suddenly," I say, changing my mind.

"No, that's okay, I totally understand," she says, somewhat distracted.

"Please tell Byron and Ellen that I'll see them soon," I say, feeling bad that I didn't say a proper goodbye to them.

"I will, don't worry," she says quietly. I wait for her to continue but she doesn't.

"Is everything okay, Josephine?" My heart jumps into my chest.

What has happened now?

I don't know how much bad news I can take.

"Nicholas called," she says.

30

OLIVE

I don't think I've heard her correctly. My skin gets flushed.

Nicholas? My Nicholas? He called *her*?

"Olive, you there?"

"Yes," I mumble.

"Did you hear me?"

"Yes, of course," I say.

How? Why? What? A hundred questions rush through my head at once, but my mouth doesn't formulate a single one out loud.

"I'm not sure if you want to hear this but I didn't want to keep anything from you," she says.

"What? What did he say?"

249

"He said he wants to talk to you, but he has a new number. Do you want to know what it is?"

"Yes, go ahead." I fumble with my phone.

I don't have anything to write it down with but I manage to open the notepad on my phone and type it in.

"There's one more thing, Olive."

"Uh-huh."

"He said this number will only work until noon Pacific time. I'm not sure what that means, but that's what he said."

After we hang up, I stare at the number until it's burned into my memory. Noon is only forty-five minutes away.

I walk around in circles trying to decide what I want to do.

Five minutes ago it was a no-brainer, but now I'm having trouble deciding.

Maybe we broke up for a reason.

Maybe I shouldn't call him.

Maybe the fact that we haven't been able to speak to each other was a blessing.

My hands shake as I dial the number.

"Hi," I whisper when he answers the phone.

"Olive? Is that you?!" Nicholas' voice is excited and frantic at the same time.

A gust of wind sweeps over me and under my sweater. In less than a second, it chills me to the bone.

"How did you get her number?" I ask even though I already know the answer.

"I had that folder for a long time," he says.

"Yes, of course," I mumble.

There's a long pause and another gust of wind comes through.

I can't hear him very well and I don't want to stay out here much longer. I climb to my feet and push my way to the car.

"How are you?" I ask.

"I'm fine. How did everything go with your mother?"

"She's perfect."

"Really?"

"She is so much more than I ever expected. She was so…happy to see me."

"That's great," Nicholas says. "I'm

very happy for you. You deserve that after…"

Given everything I have done, I'm not so sure I deserve her but I appreciate him saying so anyway.

Inside the car, his voice is crisp and clear. He asks me more about Josephine and I tell him about all of the good parts.

When he asks about Owen, I gloss over the bad parts. I don't want to make this about him.

I don't want Owen to pollute one more thing in my life.

"Tell me about yourself," I say. "How are you? Where are you?"

There's a pause on the other end followed by a deep sigh.

"I saw you on the news," I say. "And online."

"Yeah," he says quietly. "Seems like everyone is looking for me."

"You don't have to tell me if you don't want to."

"I think it's better if I don't," he says.

We don't speak for a few moments.

After a few more, the silence is unbearable.

I want to see him. I want to have this conversation in real life. I want to touch him. I want to make sure that he's still alive.

"Olive, I called you because I wanted to apologize again for everything that I did. All the lies. All the half truths. You deserve a much better man than I am."

Tears start to well up in my eyes. It sounds an awful lot like a final goodbye.

"It's okay. I mean, it's not okay but it can be," I whisper through my sobs.

"I just wanted to tell you that in case… things don't end well for me."

"Don't say that. Don't ever say that."

"It's a very real possibility."

"No, it's not. You have to keep fighting. You have to keep going."

"It's hard. If I want a chance at making a clean getaway, I need to cut all ties," he says with a long sigh.

"Then do that."

"I did, but my thoughts kept coming back to you. That's why I reached out to

Josephine. I thought that maybe you met with her and she would have your number. But it was a stupid thing to do, Olive. That's the kind of thing that's going to get me arrested or killed."

I want to tell him to never call me again.

I want to tell him that to protect himself but I can't make myself do it.

"I keep thinking about you, too," I say after a moment.

"What do we do now?" he asks.

"Where are you?"

"I can't tell you."

"Yes, of course. I knew that."

"It's nothing personal. It's just for my own safety."

"Is that why this phone number won't work after noon?"

"Yes," he says. "I'm using a burner that I'm going to throw away when we hang up. I wanted to talk to you but I didn't want Josephine or anyone else to have a way to reach me or find me."

This all makes sense but it also makes my heart ache. The more we talk about logistics the more I realize that I will probably never see him again.

"Can I trust you, Olive?" Nicholas asks after another long pause.

"Yes, of course."

"Does anyone know where you are?"

I shake my head.

"Olive? I can't hear you."

"Of course, no, sorry. I'm not home right now. I'm on the road actually, I needed to clear my head."

"That's good. How do you feel about taking a long car trip?" he asks.

31

OLIVE
WHEN I HAVE TO MAKE A DECISION...

After we hang up, I stop by Walmart and buy two phones. One is cheap and disposable that I'm going to use to call him and the second is a regular smartphone that I can use to go online and check my email among other things. I write down all of the important numbers in my original phone before I leave it in my rental house.

I don't know if all of these precautions are necessary but I don't want to take anymore risks than absolutely necessary. I have no intentions of leading the police or anyone else to Nicholas.

I just want to see him one last time.

The drive north is long but breathtaking. I drive from the Southern California desert through Las Vegas and then through Utah.

There I come upon sweeping mountain ranges whose tips are already blanketed in snow. I love the wild out here. And the silence.

I drive for miles seeing no towns or people except for a few fellow drivers.

In another life, I would have probably been afraid of being so alone, but not now.

All of the nature and the lack of humanity puts me at ease. Suddenly, I can breathe a little easier.

When I get out of Utah, I drive into Idaho where the forests get thicker and the trees get taller. When I stop for some gas, I see a bald eagle circling overhead and I watch him for a while until she flies away.

I don't have that much more to go but I know that I can't make it tonight. Besides, I'm not sure if I'm ready to see Nicholas again for the first time, at night. I'm exhausted and I need some rest.

I pull into a Motel 6 and pay for a

night through bulletproof plexiglass. The room is nice enough, simple without any detail whatsoever.

I drop my bag off on the bed and head straight to the shower. The warm water feels nice on my skin and I lather my hair with the shampoo that I brought from home.

When I turn off the water, I hear a loud meowing sound coming from outside. Since the sun has dipped below the horizon, the weather has gotten much colder and I hope that cat has somewhere warm to sleep.

I wrap my hair in a towel and plop onto one of the beds. It's springy but hard enough, and at least the pillows look new. As I skip around the channels, I hear the meow again.

Again.

And again.

I put on my pajama pants, socks, and boots along with a thick sweater and a hat. The motel is a double decker with the door of each room going straight outside.

My room is on the bottom floor and

right on the edge, so I walk around the side to see where the sound is coming from. I spot a little white and gray kitten hiding underneath a piece of cardboard.

Without another thought I scoop him up and take him inside.

"What are you doing out there all by yourself?" I ask him, wrapping my arms around him. He seems to like it because he immediately starts to purr.

"You must be so hungry and cold," I say, petting him softly.

My parents didn't believe in pets (their actual statement, whatever the fuck that means) and that's why we never had any pets growing up.

After warming up in my arms, the kitten starts to meow again. I pour a little water into a bowl. He takes a few licks and then meows again.

"Okay, let's get some food," I say, putting on my coat and covering my wet hair with a hat.

Luckily, there's a convenience store at the gas station right across the street. Not wanting to leave him alone in the room or to put him outside, I take him with me.

I pick out some milk and canned tuna before I stumble upon the pet food aisle and just grab a few of their nicest cans of cat food to last him a few days. I grab a salad and a bag of pretzels for myself along with a can opener.

Back at the motel, after we both eat, we curl up together and fall asleep.

The following morning, Solly jumps on me around five in the morning and wakes me up meowing again, begging for more food. I crack open another can of food and get back in bed.

It's almost checkout time when I wake up again to a horrible smell permeating throughout the room.

"Oh, shit," I say, pinching my nose shut with my hand. I had completely forgotten that he would need somewhere to go to the bathroom and I didn't get him anything even resembling a litter box.

Solly looks up at me with a puzzled look on his face.

"Don't worry, you're not in trouble.

I'm the one who's the moron here," I reassure him.

There are no cleaning supplies or supplies of any kind so I do what I can with some paper towels and hand soap.

After straightening my hair to not make it look so much like a bird's nest after sleeping on it wet last night, I put on some makeup and throw my stuff back into my bag. Not realizing that I have no intentions of leaving him behind, Solly sits by the front door giving me the biggest sad eyes I've ever seen.

"Of course you're coming with me, you silly kitty," I say, scooping him up into my arms. "But I think you might regret your decision. We're going to be in a car for a while."

32

OLIVE
WHEN WE GO SEE HIM...

Taking a road trip is something of a rite of passage in America.

It involves leaving home, usually somewhere out east, and exploring a world outside of your comfort zone while traveling through big cities and small towns, traversing bridges and dusty roads.

One of the most beautiful things about it is that it embodies what life is about, the journey rather than the destination. It's about going somewhere but it's also about the process of getting there.

In my case, I have a faint idea of where I am going but not what is going to happen when I get there. Nicholas and I

are no longer together and this is *not* going
to be a rekindling of our relationship.

I'm going there to see him one more
time. I want to make things right between
us but not return to the way they were
before.

I'm not foolish enough to think that we
will ever be those people again.

Around noon, I drive around a huge
lake whose waters sparkle in the sunlight. I
can't help but pull over and take a selfie.
Solly, who has been sitting in my lap since
we left the motel, gets nervous by the
sudden change of environment.

"It's okay, I'm not leaving," I say. "I'm
just taking a picture."

I try to make one where we could be in
it together but he refuses to cooperate.

A few hours later, I see the sign for
Hungry Horse Reservoir. I drive over a
small bridge and go toward the
campgrounds down a gravel road that
seems to go on forever. The road is lined on
both sides by towering pine trees which on
occasion, are interspersed with meadows.

"Am I even going the right way?" I ask Solly who simply purrs in response.

I check the gas tank. At least, I have enough to drive back out in case I'm going the wrong direction.

I pass the first campground and keep going. It's further down. Ten slow miles later, I come upon a clearing.

I drive up there and look down at the reservoir below. Under the cloudless, bright blue sky, the water looks like it's dotted with millions of diamonds.

I leave Solly in the car and get out. I walk past a few pine trees and that's when I see him, sitting with his back to me on a makeshift picnic table.

He's wearing a tight, long sleeve shirt which shows off every muscle in his back.

Somehow, I had managed to forget how sexy he is and seeing him again takes me by surprise.

Okay, deep breaths, I say to myself. I start to have doubts.

What if this was a big mistake? What if I shouldn't be here?

Before I realize what I'm doing, I turn around on my heel and start to walk away.

It's not that it feels wrong to be here, I'm just not sure if I can handle saying goodbye to him again.

I step on a twig that snaps with a loud crunching sound.

"Olive? Olive?" He rushes over to me.

Wrapping his arms around me, I stand here for a few moments feeling his breath on the back of my neck.

I turn around slowly, wanting this moment to last as long as possible.

"You came," he says in disbelief.

"You're here," I whisper.

I want him to kiss me. I want to kiss him myself but the moment passes and we both pull away.

"It's so nice to see you."

"You, too," I say.

"Why were you…leaving?" he asks.

"Um." I struggle to find the right way to say it. "I actually need to check on my cat."

He tilts his head to the side. I point to the car and show him my little friend.

As soon as I open the door, Nicholas takes him into his arms and Solly starts to purr. He pets him lovingly over and over again.

"I found him outside of the motel last night. He was really cold and hungry."

"Oh, no, I'm so sorry, little guy. Well, you're here now and nothing bad is going to happen to you again."

Our eyes meet when he says that.

I take a deep breath. I wish he would say the same thing about himself. When we look at each other for a little bit too long, I am the first to look away.

"C'mon, let me show you around," he says.

I walk over to the RV and look out at the lake below. I can see the other side of the lake but not the expanse of it to the left or right of me.

"This place is huge," Nicholas says. "I've explored some of it and I've only gone around a few bends. That was before I looked up the map and realized exactly how big it is."

"It's beautiful," I say, looking at the hawk circling overhead.

He turns my attention to his RV. It's not one of those massive rigs popular with musicians who tour all over the country but it's nice. When I step on the stairs, Nicholas extends his hand to help me inside and a surge of electricity rushes through me.

There's a small kitchen to the left facing a dining room table. The driver's seat is to the right and on the far left side there's a pop-out with a queen-sized bed.

"Wow, you have everything here," I say, looking at the door leading into the bathroom. "I've never been inside one of these before."

"I like it," he says. "It makes me appreciate the simple things in life."

Out of the window, I see an older model Honda Accord.

"That's my car," he explains.

"Do you own this, too?"

"No, this was here. It's a rental, a temporary arrangement."

"So, you're not staying here?" I ask.

"I can't," he says, shrugging his shoulders. Not understanding, I furrow my brows.

"You know where it is," Nicholas says in his intense voice without missing a beat. "Once you leave, it won't be safe for me to stay here."

33

OLIVE

WHEN WE GO SEE HIM…

Once I leave. His words reverberate in my mind over and over again. There's a finality to them.

An end point.

I catch myself fighting back tears. I didn't come here to get back together with him but I never came here knowing for sure that this would be it.

Him saying that out loud is like a nail in the coffin of our relationship.

Nicholas pours me a cup of tea and we sit down at the dinette, directly across from one another.

"I like it here," I say, taking a sip of the mint tea.

"Me, too."

"I'm surprised."

"Me, too." He laughs.

"Why did you come here of all places?"

He inhales slowly and then exhales even slower. Then he looks out of the window. "It could be that being out here in the middle of nowhere makes me hard to find," he says. "But the truth is that I needed to get away. After all of that extravagance, I needed to reconnect with nature just a bit."

"Well, you're definitely doing that."

"I needed to feel like a person again. There have been a few people camping up here but everyone really sticks to themselves. It's nice."

I ask him more about what happened after he left and he fills me in on the details.

"When we talked about running away, this was definitely not what I had in mind," I say with a smile.

"Yeah, no five-star hotels or luxury

restaurants and resorts for me. At least, not for a while."

"You think that will ever change?" I ask and he just shrugs.

When we get hungry, he toasts some garlic bread over the fire.

I make a salad and we dig in. He asks about how everything has been for me and this time I tell him the whole truth and nothing but the truth.

I don't spare any details.

What would be the point? I'm probably never going to see him again so I might as well leave nothing out.

We continue to talk as the sun dips below the pine trees out west and disappears to another place in the world.

When I get cold, he offers me a sweatshirt to put on.

When Solly rubs himself on his leg, he picks him up and cradles him in his arms.

"I've never seen this part of you," I say, smiling.

"I love animals," he says. "They don't lie. They don't cheat. They only want one thing, love and that's the only thing that any of us have to give."

I nod, petting Solly on the head, too.

He closes his eyes in pleasure.

"Besides, this one is kind of special. He loves someone I happen to as well."

What did he just say? I look up at him.

"I should've said this a long time ago, Olive. I knew that I did after just a few days of being with you. And yet, I couldn't bring myself to say it. It was so stupid. I just never heard anyone say it growing up and I guess that rubbed off on me."

"What are you talking about?" I ask quietly.

"I love you, Olive. I've loved you ever since we met and I will always love you."

I swallow hard.

I stare into his deep eyes, not knowing exactly what to say back to him. No, that's not true. I know exactly what I should say. I need to tell him I love him, too. I need to throw my arms around him and press my lips to his. But something holds me back.

"You don't have to say anything back." Nicholas puts his finger on my lips when I open my mouth. "It's not about that. I just needed you to know this. This was one of my biggest regrets from our time together."

After saying the words that I have been waiting to hear this whole time, Nicholas gets up and clears the table.

He washes the dishes in the sink and offers me something else to drink.

I glance at the time and see that somehow it got to be almost nine.

I had promised myself that I would leave before it got dark, but that was ages ago.

"It's getting really late, I think I better be going."

"Are you driving back now?"

"No, I was going to stay at a motel in town."

He nods, his shoulders slope down.

"What? What is it?" I ask.

"Why don't you stay here?" he suggests.

I look him up and down. The way his shirt clings to him, I can see practically every outline of his six pack.

His shoulders are wide and strong and his forearms have clearly outlined veins. He licks his lips and I feel a flutter in my core.

When he leans on the counter, his hair falls into his face. My knees start to feel weak.

"No, that's not a good idea," I mumble.

I don't trust myself with him.

"Listen, I'm not making any moves here. It's just a long way back to town in pitch blackness. I have a tent with me. Why don't you stay in the RV and I'll sleep outside?"

"A tent?"

"Yeah, it's perfectly comfortable. I've used it a number of times when I went on overnight hikes."

I've been hiking, too, I think to myself. Did you think about me as much as I thought about you?

"Yeah, maybe I'll do that. Don't want to disturb Solly again," I say, pointing to the little ball of fur in the corner of the dinette.

Half an hour later, I am lying down in Nicholas' bed, burying myself in his scent.

He didn't have a change of sheets but I wouldn't have it any other way.

I inhale him deeply and lose myself in his aroma. I don't realize how much I've missed him until this very moment.

34

OLIVE
WHEN I WAKE UP…

I sleep soundly for a few hours but then the sound of yelping wakes me up. It startles Solly, too, because he jumps on top of me and forces me to hold him tightly. One yelp follows another and another.

"It's okay," I whisper into his ear. "It's okay. That's just some coyotes but they are very far away from here."

Before the yelping disappears over the hills, I hear the door open slightly. My heart jumps into my chest.

Who is that?

I hear the footsteps on the stairs before the door creaks and closes shut. Still holding onto Solly, I scoot to the edge of the bed and look out.

"Oh my God, you scared the shit out of me," I say, letting out a sigh.

"You're awake! I'm so sorry. I just got really thirsty and I forgot to bring some water with me."

"It's okay, no worries," I say, putting Solly on the bed and walking into the living room.

I watch him pour himself a glass and take a few big gulps.

Nicholas isn't wearing a shirt and his body glistens under the moonlight. His pants sit low on his hips, exposing that perfect v-shaped muscle group that leads down to his groin.

I lick my lips and pour myself a glass of water as well.

"I'm really sorry I woke you up," he says.

"You didn't. I actually woke up because of the coyotes."

"Yeah, they like to sing their songs late at night."

After finishing my water, I put the glass

back on the table, next to his.

"How's the bed?" he asks, perhaps trying to buy some time to stay here a little bit longer.

"It's a lot more comfortable than that motel bed I slept in last night."

"Good, I'm glad to hear that. You should get some rest."

I should turn around and head back there but I can't seem to move my feet. He should turn and walk out of the door but he doesn't make a move either. Instead, we continue standing here, next to each other, and staring into each other's eyes.

When I move my head, a strand of hair falls into my face. I tuck it behind my ear but it frees itself once again.

This time, Nicholas reaches over.

He carefully brushes his hand across my cheek and sweeps the hair back in place. When I look up at him, his hand remains there, cradling my face.

Shivers run down my back and my nipples get hard pressing against my shirt. I resist the urge to shift my weight from one foot to another out of fear or pulling my face away from his palm.

When I look up into his eyes, the man I used to know disappears.

When we first met, he was standoffish and cold, confident yet unreachable.

And now, standing here in this room in the middle of nowhere, I suddenly see the man that he really is. Without the suits, the money, or the lies, this is the man that I am in love with.

Nicholas' lips open slightly as he moves his head closer. He blinks and unlocks our eyes from each other's before tilting my head up and pushing his lips onto mine.

My mouth opens and our tongues touch. Our kiss is soft at first as we feel each other out but then we remember that old familiar dance and suddenly we are waltzing as one.

"I love you," I whisper through the kiss.

He pulls away only slightly to look at me again.

"I love you," I repeat myself again and again. "I've loved you for a long time but I could never say it out loud either. That's the main reason I came here. I couldn't live not telling you something so important face-to-face."

In my mind, my words flow smoothly and eloquently as if they are spoken by Meryl Streep, but in reality, they come out jumbled and out of control.

"I love you, too," he whispers and grabs my arm.

His fingers braid with mine and we kiss again.

He pushes me against the counter, his strong body pressing hard against my soft one.

When I let go of his hand, I run my fingers up to his neck and then into his hair. His hands make their way into my hair, pulling my chin upward with each tug.

His breaths fill my mouth until he turns my head and starts to nibble on my earlobe. With each little bite, the outline of his dick pushes harder against my pelvic bone.

His hands run up and down my body

feeling every curve and contour. Snaking up my shirt, he finds my breasts and gently cups one and then the other as he continues to devour my mouth.

The passion I feel is difficult to describe. It overwhelms my senses and makes it hard to breathe. And when I'm in the throes of it, it feels like it will never end, as if it were a waterfall filling and overfilling a small glass of water.

With one smooth motion, Nicholas pulls the shirt over my head and suddenly my breasts are exposed to the nip of the cold night. Seeing them get covered with goose bumps, he kneels down and takes one nipple into his mouth while covering the other with his hand.

"We'll have to do something to warm you up," he mumbles.

My skin may be cold but I'm not cold on the inside. In fact, my body feels like it's a furnace.

He grabs my leg and wraps it around his torso. There are still layers of clothes separating our bodies as he starts to move his hips back and forth. He watches my reaction, teasing me.

"You like that?" he asks.

All I can do is moan.

He leads me to the bedroom even though I can barely walk. I want to climb on top of him and push him deep inside of me but first things first, we're still dressed.

I tug at his drawstring and when his pants fall down, he steps out of them. Then he picks me up and tosses me onto the bed. Before I realize what is happening, he climbs on top of me, but with his head away from mine.

My legs open on their own as his lips make their way up my legs. My hands and mouth find his dick. It tastes just as good as I remember. His tongue teases my clit as his fingers swirl inside of me. Our bodies start to move as one and a feeling of euphoria overwhelms me.

He pushes me as close to the edge as possible before pulling me away.

A few moments later, he flips around and finds my mouth with his. We kiss again as he pushes his body against mine.

I love the feeling of being under him. I watch as his strong powerful shoulders move up and down with each thrust.

Our lips continue to be locked on each other's separating only when absolutely necessary. At one point, I even gasp for air, having forgotten to breathe.

When his thrusts get faster and more powerful, my body opens up for him like a flower in the morning dew.

With each move, I take him further and further inside of me never to let him go.

Suddenly, a fire is ignited. I let out a whimper and then a long moan.

He presses his body against mine and thrusts in and out of me at an even pace until a warm soothing sensation builds within me and eventually courses throughout my veins.

A few moments later, he moves in and out of me one last time before collapsing onto the bed entirely spent.

35

NICHOLAS

WHEN I WAKE UP...

We lie in each other's arms for a long time that night first sleeping and then talking about everything and anything that we had missed during our time apart.

The one thing we do not talk about is the breakup. I hope we can pretend that it never happened, but I don't dare bring it up.

When she tells me about Owen turning me in, I want to punch him.

But when I learn that he tried to attack her and even rape her, I want to kill him. People say that all the time without really meaning it, but I never have. So when I say I want him dead, that's exactly what I mean.

In the morning, I make a breakfast of pancakes and eggs and we eat at the picnic table overlooking the lake. Birds fly over our heads and a few squirrels prance near the trees. I have been in many five-star hotels but I have never been anywhere this beautiful.

When I first found this spot, I thought that I had found paradise. But when she got here, I knew that this was heaven.

"So, what do we do now?" Olive asks, taking a bite of her pancake.

"We can go on a hike together. There's a really beautiful spot about three miles out that I know you'll love."

"That sounds perfect," she says, leaning over the table and giving me a wet, maple-syrup infused kiss.

"I love you, Olive," I say when we finally pull away from each other.

"I love you, too," she whispers back. "Why haven't we said that before?"

"Because we were stupid and immature?" I suggest and she laughs.

I'm only half joking though. Not everyone gets a second chance to right a wrong and I know that I am very lucky to be in that category.

Otherwise, I would've spent my whole life regretting never having told the woman I love that I love her.

"I have to tell you something," she says, her face suddenly getting very serious.

"Tell me anything."

She shakes her head as her cheeks get flushed from embarrassment.

"Remember the Monet you gave me?" she asks. I nod, but she doesn't continue.

"It's okay, whatever it is just tell me," I push her.

"I'm so stupid," Olive says, shaking her head. "I trusted Owen to put it in a safe place. That was before any of that happened. Before I knew who he really was."

Her body starts to shake but I just put my arm around her. "It's okay. Whatever it is, we'll figure it out."

"It's gone."

"Gone?"

"Well, I don't know if it's gone but Owen is arrested and I doubt he'll ever tell me where it is now."

"It's okay," I say without missing a beat. "I'm sure we'll find it and if we don't then…it's just money. It doesn't matter as much as this."

She puts her head on my shoulder looking relieved. I guess she really thought I would be angry at her for that.

But I wasn't lying. Money used to be the only thing that mattered to me.

But with her on my arm, I realize how poor I was when I had millions to my name and how rich I am now.

I take the plates back inside and wash them in the sink. Olive dries them and puts them back on the shelf. Once the last plate is put away, I take her into my arms and kiss her again.

"What do you think about having some more fun in bed before going on that hike?" I ask.

Her eyes light up and she grabs my arms and pulls me onto the bed.

A few moments later, there's a loud thundering sound on the front door. It swings open and two men dressed in bulletproof gear rush in, pointing their guns in our faces.

"FBI! You're surrounded. Get off her slowly and put your hands up!" one of them yells.

With my heart thumping in my chest, I do as he says.

Through the window, I see four unmarked cars and at least fifteen men with FBI field jackets. The ones on the front line are using the doors to their vehicles as shields and are positioned with their guns drawn.

"Nicholas Crawford," someone says, twisting my arm behind my back. "You have the right to remain silent and refuse to answer questions. Anything you say may be used against you in a court of law."

Everything moves in slow motion.

I glance at Olive.

She is half holding her hands in the air and half trying to hold up a sheet in front of her bare breasts.

"You have the right to consult an attorney before speaking to the police and to have an attorney present during questioning now or in the future."

My eyes search for Olive's but she keeps looking away.

None of them put down their weapons until they pull me out of the RV, handcuffed and stark naked.

When they put me into the back of a car, I look back hoping to see her again.

Did she do this? Did she turn me in?

***

Thank you for reading TELL ME TO FIGHT!

I hope you enjoyed continuing Nicholas and Olive's story. Can't wait to find out what happens at the end?

One-click TELL ME TO LIE now!

There was a time when my debt was the only link we had.

There was a time when I couldn't tell him how much I loved him and he couldn't tell me.

There was a time when I thought I could never have enough money.

Now, everything is different.

Nicholas Crawford is a stranger who is becoming more strange with every moment.

I used to think I could make a life with him, but now I'm not so sure.

We have been through too much.

But then he takes a step closer.

Then he whispers something into my ear.

Then presses his lips to my mouth.

Suddenly, everything that was wrong starts to feel so right…

Read the EPIC Conclusion to the addictive TELL ME series by bestselling author Charlotte Byrd.

One-click TELL ME TO LIE now!

I appreciate you sharing my books and telling your friends about them. Reviews help readers find my books! Please leave a review on your favorite site.

CONNECT WITH CHARLOTTE BYRD

S ign up for my **newsletter** to find out when I have new books!

You can also join my Facebook group, **Charlotte Byrd's Reader Club**, for exclusive giveaways and sneak peaks of future books.

I appreciate you sharing my books and telling your friends about them. Reviews help readers find my books! Please leave a review on your favorite site.

ALSO BY CHARLOTTE BYRD

All books are available at ALL major retailers! If you can't find it, please email me at charlotte@charlotte-byrd.com

Tell me Series
Tell Me to Stop
Tell Me to Go
Tell Me to Stay
Tell Me to Run
Tell Me to Fight
Tell Me to Lie

Tangled Series
Tangled up in Ice

Tangled up in Pain
Tangled up in Lace
Tangled up in Hate
Tangled up in Love

Black Series
Black Edge
Black Rules
Black Bounds
Black Contract
Black Limit

Lavish Trilogy
Lavish Lies
Lavish Betrayal
Lavish Obsession

Standalone Novels
Debt
Offer
Unknown
Dressing Mr. Dalton

ABOUT CHARLOTTE BYRD

Charlotte Byrd is the bestselling author of many contemporary romance novels. She lives in Southern California with her husband, son, and a crazy toy Australian Shepherd. She loves books, hot weather and crystal blue waters.

Write her here:
charlotte@charlotte-byrd.com
Check out her books here:
www.charlotte-byrd.com
Connect with her here:
www.facebook.com/charlottebyrdbooks
Instagram: www.instagram.com/charlottebyrdbooks
Twitter: www.twitter.com/ByrdAuthor
Facebook Group: Charlotte Byrd's Reader Club
Newsletter

 facebook.com/charlottebyrdbooks

 twitter.com/ByrdAuthor

instagram.com/charlottebyrdbooks

Made in United States
North Haven, CT
15 April 2023

35474133R00186